Caffeine N

No Comment

Graham Smith

Fiction aimed at the heart and the head...

Published by Caffeine Nights Publishing 2018

CONDITIONS OF SALE

Published in Great Britain by

Caffeine Nights Publishing
4 Eton Close
Walderslade
Chatham
Kent
ME5 9AT

caffeinenights.com

Also available as an eBook

British Library Cataloguing in Publication Data.
A CIP catalogue record for this book is available from the British Library

ISBN: 978-1-910720-97-4

Cover design by
Mark (Wills) Williams

Everything else by
Default, Luck and Accident

For Daniel, a young man who is a constant source of pride.

Acknowledgements:

I could write a thousand words on this subject and still miss someone important, so I'm going to cop out with some broad strokes. Heartfelt thanks to my family and friends for their constant support, Joanne Craven for her sharp editorial eye, Darren and his team at Caffeine Nights, all my Crime and Publishment gang and the bloggers who work so hard to promote myself and other authors.

The whole crime fiction community, who, to a person, have been nothing but supportive, and last but by no means least, my readers. Without readers, I'm nothing more than a stenographer for the voices in my head.

No Comment

There was so many things I was never told.

Guns N' Roses

Chapter 1

Julie Simon's eyes never wavered from the knife being held an inch from her nose. There was no tremor or shake in the knife due to the hand holding it being large, strong, and, worst of all, assured.

This could only mean one thing: the man holding the knife was calm and at peace – which told her he was comfortable with what he was about to do.

She would have screamed had a balled sock not been pushed into her mouth and secured with a strip of the same tape the two men had used to bind her to her kitchen table.

As the man sliced away the buttons of her cardigan, life in the kitchen went on as normal. The clock above the fridge ticked, the potatoes bubbled and the smell of a homemade steak pie filled the air.

The men weren't going to rape her. She was sure of that. The questions they'd asked her had told her as much.

Like all good mothers, she'd done everything she could to cover for her son – even though she didn't know why the questions were being asked.

The taller man had issued orders while the shorter, fatter, of the two, had carried them out. It was Fatty who'd slapped and beaten her, as Lanky had given him directions in the calm, emotionless voice of a satnav.

Yet it was Lanky who took a handful of her T-shirt, pulled it, and moved the knife towards it. She knew exactly how sharp the knife was; she had nicked her finger with it an hour before the two masked men had stormed through the back door and into the kitchen.

At first, she'd thought she was going to be robbed. Now she knew better, she'd have welcomed them in had they only been here to steal her valuables.

They were here to take something else from her: a thing with far greater value than her jewellery or TV. The iPad on the nest of tables, or the contents of her purse, could be replaced. What Lanky and Fatty were after could not.

Lanky's intent with the knife was clear. Julie swallowed down her fear and focused her full attention on her two aggressors as her T-shirt was sliced open.

Every detail about them was stored into her brain; locked into the recesses of her once formidable mind. Her memory might not be quite as good as it once was, but she was a long way from senile. Their heights, approximate weights and their accents were filed alongside eye colour, mannerisms and everything else she thought might be of interest to the police should she manage to survive this ordeal. She might not be able to see their faces because of the masks they wore, but she was determined to memorise every detail she could collect.

Her eyes widened as the coarse material of Lanky's glove smoothed her stomach, and she felt the sudden dampness of perspiration that covered her skin as her body reacted to the all-consuming fear.

Lanky was picking his spot, moving the knife until he had selected his target.

Like a surgeon, he directed his cutting tool with steady, deliberate movements designed to part flesh.

As she felt the first kiss of the knife, Julie offered silent prayers to a God she didn't believe in, and apologies to a son she had failed.

Chapter 2

Nothing about this shout made any sense to DC Amir Bhaki. His first impressions told him this was an everyday burglary or robbery that had gone wrong. The Major Crimes Team were not called out to investigate break-ins unless the sums taken crossed into five-figure territory.

Had there been a more serious case to occupy their time, this job would have been handed to one of the other teams.

The woman he'd seen carried out on a stretcher was almost as white as the sheet she lay on. The hurried movements of the paramedics, and the way their cheerfulness was forced, were as telling as a full medical report from a consultant.

He moved his gaze around the kitchen and wished he hadn't.

A large pool of blood lay on the floor. Everything that could be spilt, overturned or broken, had been.

Bhaki took care not to touch anything as he moved around.

The table was telling him a story – making him realise this shout may turn out to be something more interesting than expected.

'Sir, can you come and look at this?'

'What you found, Amir?' DI Campbell's accent was pure Glasgow and there were many times when Bhaki had to guess at what his new boss had said.

Bhaki pointed. 'Look at the bloodstain on the table.' He gave the DI a moment to look at the bean-shaped stain extending halfway across the table.

'I see it, but I don't see why you think it's so special.'

'It's odd, sir. There's no way it can be attributed to splatter, or her trying to clamber up and get help. I think she was lying on the table when she was stabbed.' Bhaki pointed at a series of blood spatters beneath the table. 'I think she was on the table and then tipped onto the floor.'

'You could be right. On the other hand, perhaps she was standing up when she was stabbed and then leaned on the table for support before she collapsed.'

Bhaki watched as Campbell went through the same thought processes he'd just experienced.

In Bhaki's mind, nobody sits still when burglars come into their home. Instinct makes you rise to your feet so you can defend or escape. There was no sign of any disability aids in the house, so it was reasonable to assume the victim was able-bodied.

Therefore, she would have been standing.

Perhaps the DI was right; maybe he was over-imagining the scene, trying to see things that weren't there. It could be that the victim had used the table to support herself until she collapsed.

If he was right though, she'd been placed on the table and stabbed. Which meant her assailants were after something other than household goods. A glance into the lounge was enough to confirm his theory. A large flat screen TV lay on its back, with fragments of ornaments embedded into its face.

Televisions were one of the first things burglars took. They could be sold anywhere to anyone and were valuable enough to be worth the effort. The fact that the TV hadn't been stolen, indicated electrical goods and jewellery weren't the primary goals.

Bhaki knew he had to stop thinking of this as a burglary. First off, because someone had been present and injured, the official term would be aggravated burglary or possibly, burglary with intent to commit GBH. The fact that the most obvious items to steal were still present only verified his thinking. The woman's attackers hadn't come to steal from her – at least not the usual things. They'd arrived with a different goal. Whether it was information or a specific item they were after, it was something he and Campbell would have to find out.

Whatever it was, it was important enough for a woman to have been stabbed. He realised the mess wasn't burglars being vindictive and trashing the place. It was more probable that the house had been searched. This suggested the aggressors were after a physical object rather than information.

He looked at Campbell, saw the side nod, and followed the DI outside. The quaint cul-de-sac was shrouded in a fine grey mist, as low clouds unleashed the kind of steady drizzle that soaks through clothes with ease.

Despite the weather, the neighbours were out in force. Some were carrying things to and from cars, others pretended to garden, but they all had their eyes fixed on the goings on at number six.

It was typical of life in suburbia that neighbours would gawp. The residents of Parkfield Close may, or may not, be close to the victim. The strength of their relationship didn't matter when it came to satisfying curiosity.

A pre-teen girl was crying and begging to be allowed in the ambulance. The paramedic relented and let her scramble in the back.

Bhaki reasoned the girl must be the woman's daughter. The initial report was that the poor kid had returned home from school and found her mother. A neighbour had heard the girl's screams and come running.

Campbell handed over the keys to the pool car they'd come in. 'Go to the hospital, see what you can learn from the daughter while they treat the mother. I'll stay here. I want to speak to the neighbour who called it in, and get a team on with the door to doors.'

Chapter 3

Even taking Tripod for a short walk was a challenge for Harry Evans at the moment. The beating he'd engineered for himself had ended up going further than he'd intended. It was supposed to be a few punches to earn a little sackcloth and ashes for a despicable act. The person he'd chosen as the distributor of his self-justice had seen things differently and had punched, kicked and stamped on Evans until he was restrained by other patrons of the pub.

As the beating was his penance for an underhand deed, Evans had offered no resistance to the punches that had rained onto his head and face. By the time he was knocked to the ground, and size twelve boots were flying towards him, he wasn't capable of doing anything but rolling into a ball and covering his head with his arms.

His aggressor had been spirited away by friends, and he'd been left to pick himself up on unsteady legs. He'd collapsed after three paces which had prompted someone to call an ambulance.

Six days later he was still tender – his body a riot of fading colour from half-healed bruises.

Evans settled himself into his seat and patted Tripod on the head. He'd got the three-legged Labrador from a rescue centre. As a pup, Tripod was run over and had lost one foreleg and part of an ear, but he was a loving dog who could judge his owner's mood better than most humans.

A beep from his phone alerted him to a message. He was wont to ignore it but, as it so often did, his natural curiosity got the better of him.

As soon as he saw the message was from Bhaki, his back straightened and he felt his pulse quicken. The young detective wouldn't text him, when he was on shift, just to see how he was. Which meant the message was something to do with the job.

Since being retired out of the force after the trial of his wife's rapist, Evans had been waiting for his injuries to heal so he could begin the consultancy role he'd blackmailed his replacement into giving him.

When he'd read the message, he settled back into his chair and thought about the woman who'd been stabbed. Bhaki's report was brief and to the point, as always, but more than anything, the question that followed it was the one thing other than Tripod that he had left to get out of bed for.

There had been job offers, but none offered the excitement or prestige of being a roving detective inspector in charge of a hand-picked team. His thrills had always been supplied by the puzzle, the following of clues and evidence until he could secure a conviction. The fact he knew so many people in Cumbria, along with their various connections to each other, had given him an edge no other copper in the county had.

While he had more complaints against his name than any two other members of Cumbria's finest, he could always defend himself with arrest and conviction records that echoed the complaint statistic.

He was astute enough to know Bhaki was using him; that his knowledge was being mined yet again. That didn't matter to him, it wasn't even a factor in his willingness to help. Sure, he'd grumble about it for the sake of form, but that would be the only reason.

His mouth was teased into a grin, even as his brow furrowed.

Julie Simon was a name he knew, but he didn't know much about her. From what he could recall, she'd been widowed a few years ago and left to bring up a couple of kids.

She was a decent enough woman who'd done her best to bring up the kids without a father. To the best of his knowledge, she'd never looked to replace her husband, but there was no way he could be sure if this was still true.

He'd heard something about the boy getting himself into trouble but couldn't remember specific details. He supposed it would be the usual things young teens did: petty vandalism or a spot of graffiti; a bottle of cheap cider and a spliff in either Rickerby or Bitts Park. There may have been the odd instance of shoplifting, but he couldn't see the boy's mother bringing him up to be a real problem to society. Like so many others, he'd experience the rites of passage to adulthood without crossing the line too far.

There was always the chance he'd be wrong in his assessment of the lad. He knew better than to assume that a good family meant he was a good citizen. Some of the most evil people he'd encountered were from decent families. They would present one face to the world and another to their victims. Their status in life a shield they would hide behind until it was time to swing a sword in private.

Chapter 4

Bhaki parked as close as he could to A&E and dashed in. The ambulance had been on blues and twos all the way from Parkfield Close. Harry Evans may have managed to keep pace with it in the M3 he used to have, but there was no way he was even going to try in a diesel Astra.

The reception was quiet with only a smattering of people waiting to be seen. An elderly woman had a blood-stained teacloth wrapped around one hand, and a young mother cradled a whimpering baby while a young boy snuggled into her side. The lump on the boy's head was threatening to close one eye, although he was being brave and fighting his tears back.

He flashed his warrant card at the receptionist and enquired where he might find Julie Simon.

A minute later he was being led through to the cubicles where patients are assessed. The receptionist poked her head through the curtain and recoiled an instant later.

The curtain was pulled back and a team of grim-faced doctors wheeled a stretcher out. Julie Simon's daughter trailed after them with tears running down her face in thick rivulets.

Bhaki followed a pace or two behind the procession. There was no doubt in his mind Julie was being rushed to an operating theatre.

After forty yards his guess was proven right.

The girl didn't see it, but a doctor nodded to a nurse and then her. The nurse peeled away and blocked the girl's path.

'I'm sorry, sweetheart, but you can't go in there. You'll have to stay out here with me.'

The girl tried to sidestep the nurse without success. 'Let me past. My mum needs me.'

'She does, sweetheart. But right now she needs those doctors to be able to do their job.' The nurse's tone was patient and calm without being condescending. 'You can't go in there because you haven't been scrubbed down. You wouldn't want your mum's recovery to be affected by an infection, would you?'

The girl's head shook, and then she crumpled against the nurse. Now the adrenaline rush of the ambulance ride and the race along a corridor were over, her body was shaking with fear, grief and a chemical reaction to stress.

Bhaki caught the nurse's eye, and gave her a long look at his warrant card, as he kept his face in a friendly yet helpful pose.

'Sweetheart, I need to go and help the doctors—.'

'Noooooooo.'

The nurse crouched until her face was level with the girl's. 'Don't worry, sweetheart, I'm not going to leave you alone. My friend is here and he's going to sit with you while we get your mum all fixed up. Amir is a policeman, so anything you can tell him will help him to catch whoever did this to your mum.' Somehow the nurse managed to paint a smile on her face. 'The paramedics said you were very good at answering their questions. Said you being so clever really helped them. Do you think you can be clever again to help Amir catch the man who stabbed your mum?'

The girl's head nodded once.

Bhaki gave the nurse a smile and mouthed his thanks as she straightened up. The woman's intelligent handling of the girl had just made his job a lot easier.

He kept his smile in place as the girl turned around to face him. 'Hi there. I'm Amir, what's your name?'

The girl eyed him with suspicion. 'Will you really catch the man who did this to my mum?'

'I'll do everything I possibly can.' Much as he wanted to say yes to the girl, he preferred to be honest with her. She looked old enough to understand how the world works and he didn't want to get off on the wrong foot with her by making false promises. 'My boss is at your house and he'll have already started the investigation. He's sent me here to look after you and to ask you a few questions.' He tried another smile. 'You never did tell me your name.'

'It's Gracie.' Her voice fell to a whisper. 'Will my mum be okay?'

'She's in the best possible place.' His smile faded as he thought of Janet Evans. 'I knew the lady who used to be in charge of Accident and Emergency. She and her team saved many people's lives.'

The only answer he got from Gracie was a sob.

He cursed himself for his tactless words. The suggestion her mum's injuries may prove fatal should never have been voiced.

'In your own time, Gracie, can you tell me what you found when you got home?'

A whimpered sob was followed by a huge sniff as Gracie took control of her emotions. Tears still leaked down her face as she spoke in a wavering voice, but her account was as clear as Bhaki could hope for in the circumstances.

'I got home from school and dumped my bag on the table. I was going to get a biscuit and a drink, like, you know, before I did my homework.' A pause to swallow and maintain her self-control. 'When I went into the kitchen I found her lying on the floor.' A sniffle. 'Oh my God there was blood everywhere.'

Gracie's sniffles turned back into sobs.

'What did you do next?' Bhaki could see blood on the girl's knees from where she must have gone to help her mother, but he needed to hear her account.

'I'm not sure. Linda from next door just appeared and started cuddling me. I know there was screaming, but it wasn't coming from Linda. Or mum.' Gracie's eyes widened as she realised she was the one the screams had come from.

Bhaki gave her a moment to piece the events together in her mind.

'Who phoned for the ambulance, was it you?'

'It was Linda. She was holding me. Pulled me away from mum when she was on the phone.' Shame, and a little fear darkened Gracie's face. 'I called her some nasty names when she wouldn't let me go to help mum.'

'I'm sure she'll understand.' Bhaki used a curled forefinger to lift her chin. 'She did the right thing not letting you near your mother. Sometimes people who try and help can do more harm than good if they haven't had the proper training.'

'Is she going to be okay?'

Bhaki silenced the sigh before it got to his mouth and opted for honesty. 'I'm sorry, Gracie, I'm a policeman, not a doctor. I really can't answer that question any better than you can.'

The nod she gave him told Bhaki he'd struck a chord by treating her as an adult. For him, pre-teens were foreign territory. His sister had a couple of boys under three who could always be amused with peek-a-boo and silly voices. A young girl on the cusp of puberty was something else. Add the shock she'd had in finding her mum in a pool of blood, and his chances of striking up a rapport were slimmer than ever. The best he could hope for was not upsetting her while getting as much information as possible.

A rumble from his stomach cut through the air.

'Excuse me.' He felt his cheeks warm. 'That's not very professional is it?'

A shrug.

'You said you were going into the kitchen for a biscuit, Gracie. You must have been hungry.' He gestured towards the reception area. 'There's a vending machine back there. Shall we go and get a bar of chocolate or some crisps? We can get a tin of coke as well.'

'I'm not hungry now.'

'Maybe you're not feeling hungry, but your body will still need the energy that food gives it.'

Her eyes fixed on the door of the operating theatre. 'I'm not hungry.'

'C'mon, we'll only be a minute. As soon as you've chosen what you want, I'll get it while you come back here.' He didn't want to overplay his hand and turn her against him. 'Don't worry, one of the nurses will come looking for us if we're not there.'

A look at the door again and she was off marching towards the vending machines.

Bhaki followed at her heel and stayed true to his word. She pointed out two bars of chocolate and a bag of crisps before asking him to also get her a bottle of water.

He fed money into the machines and doubled up her order. What she didn't eat, he would.

Upon returning to the corridor by the operating theatre, he checked his phone while Gracie munched on a bar of chocolate. Neither Evans nor Campbell had messaged him. For the time being, he was an ill-equipped nursemaid to a frightened child who was trying her best to act like an adult.

'So, Gracie.' As she opened a bag of crisps, he sipped a bottle of water and questioned her about her mum. He asked the usual questions such as her age, and what she did for a job. It was when he moved on to Gracie's father things took a different turn.

'He's dead.' The thin voice was matter of fact. 'He died in an accident at work when I was a baby. I never knew him at all.'

Bhaki's heart ached for the young girl. Here she was, sitting outside an operating theatre with a stranger who was peppering her with questions; while on the other side of the wall, doctors were fighting to save her one remaining parent's life.

The fact she could do anything but cry spoke of Gracie's inner fortitude. He couldn't imagine what it must be like to grow up without ever knowing a father. To face the possibility of losing her mother as well must be terrifying for her.

He imagined himself in her position. Couldn't tell himself he'd be as composed as she was; couldn't see himself not dissolving into a mass of tears and wails.

A thought struck him. 'Do you have any brothers or sisters?'

'A brother.'

There was enough hesitation in her answer to pique his interest, although it could be nothing more than typical sibling rivalry.

'What time does he normally get home?' Bhaki was thinking he could give Campbell a heads up that the son was expected home, when he realised a horrible truth. Most attacks in the home were committed by a family member. It was entirely possible Gracie's brother had lashed out, in a moment of teenage angst, and stabbed his mother.

If that was the case, the boy had likely panicked and run off somewhere. They would need to find him before he did a complete disappearing act, or got himself into more trouble.

'He won't be coming home. Not for a long time.' Once again fat tears rolled down Gracie's cheeks.

Bhaki suspected she knew something about her mum's injury and had to fight to keep the excitement from his tone. 'Why not?'

Gracie's eyes found her shoes and locked on them. 'Because he's gone away. We are allowed to go and visit him, like, but I hate seeing him there. Mum always makes me wear trousers or jeans when I want to wear a dress to look nice for him. She says that she doesn't want anyone else there looking at my legs.' She sniffled. 'Mum always cries when it's time for us to leave. Sometimes Jack does too.'

The excitement Bhaki had felt was now an ominous sinking feeling.

'I take it Jack is your brother?'

A nod.

'Where is he at?'

'Deerbolt.'

Bhaki recognised the name. Deerbolt was a young offenders institution, over at Barnard Castle in County Durham.

Chapter 5

The coffee he was handed was strong and bitter – just the way he liked it. Campbell was sat in a kitchen with a layout identical to Julie Simon's in every way.

'You say you ran next door when you heard screams. Can you tell me what you found?'

Linda took a sip of her coffee and blinked away a tear. 'When I went in, Julie was lying on the floor and Gracie was bent over her. The poor lass was screaming and trying to pick up her mother. I pushed her back and pressed a towel over the wound on Julie's stomach. And then I called an ambulance.'

'Okay. Now I want to walk you through this step by step. Was the back door open when you entered?'

'No.' A moment's thought. 'It wasn't locked though.'

'Does Mrs Simon usually leave her door unlocked?'

'I'm not sure. I tend to lock mine after having tea.'

Her words made sense to Campbell. The cul-de-sac looked respectable enough, but it was only a stone's throw from the nearby Harraby estate.

Evans and the rest of the team had told him about the various areas of Carlisle when he'd transferred to the Major Crimes Team from Glasgow. Harraby had improved since a low point in the nineties, but there were still enough troublesome families who'd think nothing of petty burglary, robbery or assault. These families would always have a member or two willing to join the ranks of whichever gang ran the crime in their area.

In Carlisle's case, the Leighton family held all the cards, and the head of the family, Maureen, was astute enough to only deal the hand she wanted others to have.

If Bhaki's assumption was right, Julie's stabbing could be the result of, or precursor to, something far more serious than assault with a deadly weapon. First though, he had to make sure it wasn't a typical domestic argument which had got out of hand.

Campbell thought about his elder sister's experiences of child rearing. She'd told him his two nephews had become argumentative, and how they would challenge every word she said to them as soon as they went to secondary school.

Gracie would be around the same age. Hormones would play a huge part of it, as would the natural pushing of boundaries. He didn't want to think she had stabbed her mother in some over-emotive fight, but if he didn't consider it he'd be neglecting his duty.

Gracie looked old enough to start arguing back, although, when she'd climbed into the back of the ambulance all maturity had been washed from her face, leaving her looking like the scared child she was. The question he had to answer was: was Gracie scared for her mother or for the consequences of her own actions?

As improbable as it seemed, that Julie had allowed her daughter to assault her before the girl managed to pick up a knife, it wasn't beyond the bounds of possibility. Still, his gut was telling him the girl was innocent even while his experience insisted she may not be.

'So, you enter through the unlocked door and see Julie and Gracie on the kitchen floor. Stop yourself by the door and tell me everything you see.'

Linda's eyes closed as she revisited the scene.

'There was something cooking on the stove. There was a nice smell in the air – until I saw Julie on the floor. As soon as I saw the blood, that was all I could smell.'

'Very good. What else could you see?'

'Gracie was cuddling her mother and screaming. I pulled a towel from where it had been looped through a drawer handle, and balled it against Julie's wound.' A tearful shrug. 'Other than calling for an ambulance, I didn't know what else to do.'

Campbell gave an emphatic nod. 'Not many people do in such circumstances. You did the right thing though. I only know a limited amount of first aid, but what I do know tells me you should try to stem the blood flow and not move the patient. You did both, so well done.'

As well as offering the woman reassurance, Campbell was using the praise as a way to ingratiate himself with her. The friendlier she thought him, the more she would tell him.

'Until Julie gets examined at the hospital we won't know for sure but, by all appearances, it would seem she was stabbed. Did you see a bloody knife anywhere?'

The question was crucial. Many times a well-meaning neighbour or family member had tidied up a crime scene and destroyed evidence.

'No.' A definite shake of the head. 'There were a couple of knives on the draining board, but I didn't see one covered with blood.'

Campbell hadn't seen one either. Which meant that the attacker had taken the knife away. This was probable, and even likely, if the knife used was their own. If they'd picked one up in the kitchen there was a chance they'd washed it and left it behind, or taken it away to be dumped in a random wheelie bin or drain, or tossed into a river.

Another detail came back to him. 'Was it you who switched the cooker off?'

'Yes. I didn't touch anything else, but I thought it best to turn off the oven and the hobs – I didn't want anything to catch fire.'

'That's fine. You didn't do anything wrong by switching them off.'

Campbell thought about his next moves. He'd called out a pair of crime scene investigators, but couldn't allocate a greater portion of his budget until he knew more details. A sad fact of modern policing was that budgets controlled investigations as much as detectives did. Should Julie die of her injuries, more money would become available. As frustrating as this reality was, there was nothing Campbell could do about it.

'Okay. Leading up to the time before you heard Gracie screaming, did you hear any shouting; an argument? Things being smashed?'

'I'm sorry, but I was out. I'd just got back when I heard the screams.' She pointed to a supermarket carrier bag, lying on a worktop, with groceries spilling out.

'How about things in general, do they argue often? Gracie looks as if she's getting to that awkward teen stage.'

A fond smile caressed Linda's lips. 'If they argue, it's not what you'd call a big argument. They dote on each other and are as close as can be.' A darker expression replaced the smile. 'When Jack was here, there were arguments.'

'Who was Jack? Her husband?'

'No her son. He went away a few months ago.'

'What about her husband or boyfriend.' Campbell glanced at his watch. 'When are they likely to be back?'

'She a widow. Her husband died in an accident just after Gracie was born. As far as I know, Julie isn't seeing anyone, but she's very coy about such things; doesn't tell me much, if anything.'

'Do you know where her son went?'

'No. I just stopped seeing him. I figured he'd moved away to college or had gone to live with a relative rather than stay at home.'

'What about her family, do you know how I could get in touch with some of them?'

'Sorry, no.'

Campbell finished his coffee, thanked her and went outside to check his mobile for messages. While speaking to Linda he'd felt its vibrations in his pocket. The fact it hadn't rung meant none of the team had unearthed a strong lead.

He put a call in to DS Neil Chisholm, who acted as the team's hub. A computer whizz, he searched the databases, scanned reports and collated the various information they gathered.

For Chisholm, locating other members of Julie's family would be a simple task. Campbell had an especial interest in the son and wanted to know more about him.

With the call made, Campbell looked around and saw DC Lauren Phillips leaving a house on the other side of the cul-de-sac.

He called her over and listened to what she had to say. It was much the same as everything he'd got from Linda.

'C'mon, we'll go see what the CSI boys have found.'

Chapter 6

As the time passed, without anyone emerging from the operating theatre, Bhaki found it harder and harder to reassure Gracie.

He'd exhausted all lines of questioning with her. What he'd learned was of little use. She and her mother got along well. The one bone of contention in their relationship was her mother's refusal to tell her why Jack was in Deerbolt.

All the male young offenders in the area were sent to Deerbolt when given custodial sentences. Like all such institutions, it was a place where the strong preyed on the weak. Where futures were mapped out according to the level of each individual's fear of returning. For some, it would be a training ground; for others a recruitment centre.

There would be a third group, they'd be the ones who'd made one silly mistake and were paying the full price for it. Every night they'd cry into their pillows, and be thankful it was one less day they'd have to spend away from their parents. These were the inmates who'd make damn sure they never returned. Most of this group would be abused and humiliated on a daily basis by the tougher, less advantaged, inmates for whom spending time in a young offenders institution was inevitable from birth.

While he suspected Jack would fall into the latter category, there was no way of telling if he was right until DS Chisholm looked up the boy's record.

The questions he'd asked Gracie about Julie's love life had been met with an icky expression, as the girl showed her distaste at the idea of her mother having sex.

To the best of the girl's knowledge, there was no current boyfriend and she'd never known her mother to go on a date. While it was possible she'd been shielded from this aspect of her mother's life, Bhaki wasn't sure that was the case. Gracie was a sensible girl and it was a long time since her father had died.

However, like everyone else on the planet, Julie Simon would have needs. Sexual desires. While she may have devoted herself to bringing up her children, apps like Tinder made casual – no-strings-attached – sexual encounters easy to arrange.

If Julie was as pretty as her daughter, she wouldn't lack male attention. It could be a neighbour she was seeing. A married man who'd never commit to her may be the perfect solution. They could hook up for sex, once or twice a month, as the opportunity arose. Neither expecting anything more from the liaison than a satisfying of needs.

Should this be the case, there was a strong possibility that the person who wielded the knife was a jealous wife or girlfriend.

It would be hard to learn this person's identity unless Julie had confided in someone. A sister or a girlfriend may know.

He'd sent all his findings to DI Campbell by text, and sent the same information to Harry Evans.

His ex-guv would know he was being used but would help them regardless. With Evans, the only thing that mattered was the delivering of justice. He'd used any method he could and trampled over feelings without a care, and he'd expected the same from his team.

'Gracie, how are you, lass?'

The voice interrupted his reverie. When he looked up he saw a tearful woman, accompanied by a stoic man.

Gracie dashed from her chair and threw herself into the arms of the woman. 'Auntie Wendy.'

'Shush now. Don't cry. Remember when Jack was poorly a couple of years ago and the doctors here made him all better? That's just what they're doing for your mum right now.' Wendy cradled her niece. 'You did very well remembering our number and getting this policeman to call us.'

Bhaki could see the back of Gracie's ears redden as she took the praise on board. He extended a hand towards the stoic man. 'DC Bhaki.'

'Martin Harper.' The handshake was firm, but Harper's skin was clammy and Bhaki's eye was never met.

With the girl taken care of, Wendy's concern shifted to her sister. 'Has there been any news? How's Julie?'

Bhaki spread his hands wide in the universal gesture of helplessness. 'Sorry, but we've not heard anything since she was taken into theatre.'

'She's not going to die, is she?'

As Wendy consoled her niece, Bhaki couldn't help but notice she used the same non-committal reassurances he had.

All four heads turned at the whispering sound of the operating theatre door opening. The kindly nurse stepped out and closed the door behind her before any of them could look inside.

She stepped towards Gracie and bent to her level. 'Sweetheart. I'm very happy to tell you your mum has come through the operation. She'd lost a lot of blood, but the doctor has got her all fixed up—.'

Gracie interrupted the nurse with a huge bear hug. 'Thank you, thank you, thank you.'

'Easy, sweetheart. Your mummy is still very weak and the doctor's got her under observation at the moment. In a little while we'll be moving her to the intensive care unit. Another group of doctors and nurses will look after her there until she's well enough to go on to a general ward.'

Wendy stepped forward. 'Can we see her?'

'Not at the moment. She's still in recovery.' The nurse gave a wide smile and stood up, but kept her eyes on Gracie. 'I'm sure that you can accompany her when she's moved to ICU though. The doctor will be out soon to tell you more, but I wanted to let you know as soon as possible that your mum is going to be okay.'

She beckoned Bhaki to one side. 'The surgeon wants to see you too.'

Intrigued, Bhaki sat back down and waited with Gracie and her aunt and uncle. The girl's mood had undergone a radical change now she knew her mother was going to survive. There were still tears flowing down her cheeks, but they were now happy ones.

He listened with half an ear as Wendy started planning how they would manage Julie's hospital stay. The rest of his attention was on what the doctor may tell him.

Bhaki tried his best to guess what he'd be told but couldn't think of anything which made any sense. It didn't surprise him – his career as a detective might be short when compared to the likes of Evans, or even Campbell – but if there was one thing he'd learned, it was to never expect things to be straightforward.

Chapter 7

Campbell slung his damp jacket over the back of his chair and turned to look around the room. He'd got the whole team assembled and this was their first real case without the all-pervading influence of Harry Evans. He wanted them to get a quick result so he could start proving his worth to the brass.

As Evans' replacement, his mandate had been spelt out to him with a crystalline clarity. Not only was he expected to maintain the high arrest and conviction rates enjoyed by his predecessor, he was to instil the team with a new ethos which put an end to their renegade ways.

Some of the team would be easier to manage than others. Bhaki was the newest recruit and, while he looked up to Evans, he was unfailing in his politeness, diligent and more amenable than the other two.

DC Lauren Phillips would be more problematic. Her good looks and flirtatious behaviour were all part of her armoury. She thought nothing of popping a button or two open, or revealing a stocking top if it would distract a suspect into making a foolish admission, or keep a solicitor's mind off their job. On top of that, she was a comfortable rule-breaker who only followed protocol when it furthered her cause. Her greatest skill was in the interview room: with her diversionary tactics and quick mind, she could trick even the most stubborn 'no-commenter' into saying the wrong thing.

The final member of the team was DS Neil Chisholm. A computer expert who could access any database necessary. He treated firewalls and security systems with contempt as he traversed the digital highways looking for whatever information the team needed. While he could point the team in the right direction, at least half of his findings were inadmissible in court.

Campbell might have only been in charge of the Major Crimes Team for a fortnight, but he'd already found himself fudging the details of Chisholm's digital excavations when reporting to DCI Grantham.

'Right then.' Campbell took up position by the whiteboard, which adorned one wall of their tiny office. 'We have one Julie Simon, age thirty-nine, stabbed in the stomach in her own home.

She was widowed eleven years ago, has a twelve-year-old daughter, Gracie, who lives with her, and a son, Jack, sixteen, who's currently in Deerbolt YOI. Nothing would appear to have been stolen from her house as all the usual targets haven't been taken. Therefore, I'm thinking the attack is personal rather than just her disturbing random burglars. CSI will give us their report as soon as they can.' He pointed a marker at Lauren and fought to keep the disappointment from his voice. 'Tell the others what you got from the neighbours.'

'According to everyone I spoke to in the cul-de-sac where she lives, Julie Simon is a decent woman who is a good neighbour and is easy to get on with. None of them knew of any scandal or trouble affecting her. They all assumed her son had gone off to college or moved to live with another family member, as not one of them mentioned he was in Deerbolt.'

'If we're going down the personal route, was she seeing anyone?'

'Good question, Neil. She wasn't according to those I spoke to.' Campbell pointed his marker at Lauren again. 'What about you?'

'I asked, but they said she was single as far as they knew.' Lauren gave a shrug. 'Perhaps she didn't advertise it. She could be knocking off one of the neighbours on the sly or seeing a guy from the other side of town and only meeting him at his place because she's thinking of her kids.'

Chisholm shook his head at them. 'If you get me her mobile, I'll have his name, address and inside leg measurement within an hour.'

'I'm on it.' Lauren picked up her phone. 'What about the son, could it be something to do with the reason he's in Deerbolt?'

'I doubt it.'

Campbell whirled to face Bhaki. The young detective's tone had been sure. 'Why not?'

'I spoke to his aunt and uncle at the hospital. 'He was caught in possession of enough ecstasy tablets and cannabis to earn him a stay at Her Majesty's pleasure. He denied it and said it was planted in his locker, but nobody had believed him except his mother.' Bhaki grimaced. 'The aunt said he'd refused to say who he thought had planted it.'

It was a familiar story. A school child would be lured into dealing drugs in the playground. When they were inevitably caught, they didn't have the nerve to tell anyone who supplied them. Enough threats would have been made against their family members to ensure they were more frightened of their suppliers than a stay in any young offenders institution.

'It looks like a dead end, but I think it still bears looking at now his mother's been attacked. Did the aunt say anything else?'

'Just that she's going to look after Gracie until her mother is home and well.' Bhaki hesitated. 'I also asked her if she knew if Julie was seeing anyone. She said not as far as she was aware.' Another hesitation. 'I was looking at the uncle as she was speaking. He looked decidedly shifty when I was asking about the victim's sex life.'

'Interesting.' Campbell felt his lips pulling into a smile. 'I think Lauren and I should have a word with him tomorrow, when we can separate him from his wife.'

'There's more, sir. The surgeon who operated on Julie had a word with me.'

'What for?'

Campbell gave Bhaki his complete attention, and was aware of Lauren and Chisholm doing the same.

'She said she'd never seen a wound quite like it.'

'In what way?'

Campbell scowled at Lauren for the interruption. 'Go on, Amir.'

'She said the wound went straight into Julie's actual stomach, not just her belly.' Bhaki grimaced in distaste. 'She said the stomach wall showed signs of tearing, as well as having been cut.' Another grimace. 'She said that it was as if someone had forced the initial wound open.'

Campbell's stomach flipped, and not in a good way, as he digested what Bhaki was saying. An A&E surgeon would be more than familiar with stab wounds. If she said Julie Simon's wound was like none she'd seen before, then it could have a direct bearing on the case.

'Did she offer any theories?'

Bhaki shook his head. 'She didn't want to speculate. I tried pushing her, but she got called away to another patient.'

'Fair enough. Follow it up tomorrow morning, see if she's got any ideas when she's had time to think about it.' Campbell turned to Chisholm. 'Neil, get what you can from Julie's phone and have a look into her life, please. I want to know her income, her record – if she has one, and anything else you can uncover without hacking into places you shouldn't.'

Chapter 8

Evans' body ached as he levered himself from his chair. Whoever had decided to knock on his door at this time of night would have to wait until he limped across the hall.

Another knock.

'I'm coming, you impatient fucking imbecile.' He kept his voice loud enough to be heard without raising it enough to disturb his neighbours.

He opened the door to find Lauren standing there, with an amused twist to her expressive mouth. 'If I'm an imbecile, you must be a dickhead for keeping me on your team. Here.' She pushed the pizza box she was carrying towards him. 'I don't expect you'll have eaten.'

As he led her into the lounge, he did everything he could to disguise the aches that were torturing his body.

'First a message from Bhaji Boy, and now a visit from you. I take it DI Jock McJock is stumped and you've come here expecting me to bail you out of the shit?'

'You could take it that way. You could also take it that a concerned friend, who spent a night sitting by your hospital bed, has dropped in to see how you are. Or, you could take it that I've come to share confidential details of a case with you, in an effort to give you something to think about other than your own misery and self-pity.'

Evans dropped his eyes to the pizza box. After a few seconds of showing contrition, he opened it and saw the proliferation of pepperoni slices and abundance of jalapeno peppers.

'Thanks.'

He wasn't just thanking her for the pizza, but she was smart enough to know that.

'Do you want your Tabasco sauce?' She rose to her feet.

'Please. There's a bottle of wine in the fridge if you want a glass.'

He took the bottle of fiery sauce from Lauren and sprinkled a liberal amount over his pizza. The first bite he took inflamed his mouth and left a tingle on his lips.

Lauren sat a mug of tea down in front of her and looked at the glass sitting on the table by his chair. There was no condemnation on her face but he felt the need to explain anyway.

'Don't worry. I'm not about to climb inside a bottle. That's my first, and I was asleep in the chair when you arrived anyway.'

'Your life.'

'Enough with the bullshit small talk. Do you want to tell me about the case?'

As she spoke, Evans kept stuffing large bits of pizza into his mouth. This was what he loved: the puzzle, the challenge of pitting his wits against those of the wrong-doers, but most of all, he loved the way a successful investigation allowed him to deliver justice.

He sucked his fingers clean and then wiped them dry on his trousers. 'So, you think the stabbing is connected to either her sex life or the boy's drug dealing?'

'Pretty much.' She gave a helpless shrug. 'Unless you have a better idea?'

'Both of those scenarios are plausible, apart from one thing.' He looked at her, willing her to make the connection herself.

'The wound?'

'Bingo. The fact she has internal tearing suggests only one thing to me. After the knife was removed, something else was put inside her. Something larger than the knife. This object is what forced the wound to open and therefore caused the walls of her stomach to tear.'

'According to Amir, the surgeon never mentioned a foreign object being found inside her.'

'It may have only been inserted to cause her pain.' Evans paused to light a cigarette and thought for a moment. 'If it was connected to the boy, she would have been killed outright or given some kind of punishment we'd recognise. If it was retribution, then whatever was put into her stomach would have been left there to send a message.'

'So you think it's to do with her sex life?'

'I can't say for sure, but it speaks more of a twisted vengeance than a gang punishment to me.' A disgusting idea entered his mind. 'If I was a betting man, I'd say that she'd been found out by the wife, or girlfriend, of someone who's been shagging her on the sly, and that's who stabbed her. Then, to further the punishment, she's had some kind of dildo or sex toy shoved into her wound.'

Lauren's mouth twisted into a distasteful sneer. 'That's bloomin' sick, guv.'

'I'm not saying it isn't, but there are lots of sick people out there. Let's be honest, if she'd been undressed, you'd be wondering if she'd been raped. This may be a different kind of rape.' He made sure he caught her eye. 'You know yourself how some people can flip when they find out their partner is cheating. Remember that big fracas at the Crown and Mitre last year; how it all kicked off because one bridesmaid caught her husband getting a blowjob from another?'

'Yeah. What was the final count there?'

'Two stabbings, one person hospitalised for a week, seventeen arrests and a dozen people charged. And that all happened when one woman went a bit tonto because her husband was cheating on her.'

'Point taken.' Lauren picked up her mug. 'C'mon then, guv, what do you suggest?'

'You're looking at the sister's husband aren't you? Imagine how angry the sister would be if Julie was sleeping with her husband. I suggest you have a very close look at her too. Get Jabba to find out if she suffers from depression, or has anger management issues.'

'That might be a problem. DI Campbell has already told him not to go anywhere he shouldn't.'

'What he doesn't know won't hurt him. Just make sure he doesn't find out and you'll be fine. It will also mean you know if you're barking up the wrong tree. Or at least if you're in the right forest.'

The smile she failed to keep hidden told him she'd do as he suggested. Campbell was all about modern policing and would follow procedure, whereas he always followed his gut.

Evans yearned to have a greater involvement in the case; longed to look into someone's eyes across the table in an interview room and determine whether or not they were lying. Yet, until Campbell requested his services as a consultant, he'd have to stay on the fringes and feed on the scraps his old team tossed him.

'So, guv. How have you been?'

'Fine, fine.' He waved a hand. 'Been doing a bit of reading. Taken Tripod on a few walks. Think I'll start sorting out Janet's things in a couple of days. There's a lot of good stuff a charity shop could make a few quid from.'

He hoped she'd get the subtext. Would understand that he was still healing in mind and body; that he needed to busy himself when he recovered from the beating; that he'd do things at his own pace when he was ready for each step. Most of all he wanted her to recognise that he was beginning to take steps to adjust to his new life as a widowed ex-detective inspector.

'Sounds like you've got plenty to keep you occupied.' Her smile faded and she gave him a little nod. 'If you need help with any of it, don't think twice about asking. I'm sure I can rope in Amir and DS Chisholm to help lug any boxes as well.'

Evans didn't know what to say, didn't trust his voice to retain its normal strength. All he wanted to do was give Lauren a big hug and say thank you.

As ever, he retreated behind a gruff exterior rather than show his true feelings. 'What, do you think I'm not able to put a few dresses into a bag? That I'm too old to sort out her stuff by myself? D'you think I'm so soft that I'll fall apart every time I see summat that reminds me of her? I'm Harry Evans. The He-Man. I'll be fine.'

'I know exactly who you are, you cantankerous old bugger. That's why I'm offering to help you.'

Evans hadn't expected her to fall for his bluster, she was too smart and knew him too well, but he didn't dare let his guard down in front of her. Once down, it could never again be raised. All he had left was pride. Pride in himself and an overwhelming pride in his team.

'I'll be fine, lass. Some things have to be faced and I'm not daft enough to face them until I'm ready.'

Chapter 9

Campbell glanced around the graphic design studio. The walls were adorned with examples of completed projects and there were two men and one woman absorbed in their computer screens. All three were dressed in casual clothes, and there was a muted radio playing in the background as text was enlarged and pictures were cropped or enhanced.

When Martin Harper emerged from the small office at the back of the design studio, he looked harassed and more than a little irritable. Campbell guessed, by the bags under his eyes, there had been little sleep in his household.

A hand was extended. 'You must be the detective I spoke to.'

Harper took them into his office which was also decorated with examples of his company's output.

'We're sorry to trouble you, Mr Harper. We only have a few questions and shouldn't take up too much of your time.' Campbell wanted to put the man at ease. He'd discussed tactics with Lauren and they'd decided that he should lead. She would jump in if there were any hints at evasiveness. She'd explained it was what she often used to do with Evans and was successful, more often than not, as she was underestimated.

As loathe as he was to adopt any of Evans' habits, he'd often done the same thing with a DC in Glasgow. For some reason, suspects relaxed when a DI stopped putting questions to them and a junior officer took over. It was as though the junior officer was just trying to contribute to the conversation when the reality was that they were the real threat to the suspect.

Campbell watched as Harper's eyes scanned them both as they sat on the chairs facing his desk. His sweep of Lauren took a second or two longer than was polite, and a flash of lust was visible for a fleeting moment.

Conceding home territory like this was a double-edged sword. On some occasions, familiar surroundings comforted people and made them more open. At other times it made the suspects feel superior and had them clamming up or sneering at the investigating officers.

In his opinion, there was a lot to be said for the intimidating atmosphere of an interview room.

'Our colleague, DC Bhaki, who was at the hospital with Gracie last night, said he'd asked you and your wife about your sister-in-law's attack. You both said you had no idea who was behind it. Now, obviously, we don't want to repeat the same questions he asked, but there are a few points I'd like to clear up.' Campbell gave a quick smile. 'We thought you might be the better person to ask as your wife will have Gracie with her.'

'Fair enough. What do you want to know?'

Harper's tone was even but his fingers drummed on the desk. Campbell marked it down as a possible nervous tic but was aware it could be nothing more than an annoying habit.

'First of all, can you tell us a bit more about your nephew – we understand he's in Deerbolt Young Offenders Institution. We know what for, but we'd like to hear your family's side of the story.'

'You think the attack on Julie is connected to that?' His head bobbed to one side. 'He was pretty much a good kid – if a little weird. I don't mean bad weird, just a little off kilter compared to other kids his age. I was surprised when he was caught with that amount of drugs though. He's never struck me as someone who'd get involved with them. While he was aloof and often lived in his own world, I never saw any bad in him. In fact, he doted on Gracie and would amuse her rather than hang out with lads his own age. He tried telling us the drugs were planted on him, but even when his mum asked who he thought planted them he wouldn't answer her. I'm sorry if it sounds cynical and unkind, but the fact he wouldn't tell his mother who he suspected, made me doubt his story.'

Campbell agreed with Harper's assessment, but had enough sense not to say so and alienate the man.

A drum of the fingers. 'And before you ask, no, I don't have any idea where he got the drugs, or who may have planted them. Neither did his mother.'

Campbell made a dismissive gesture. 'That's okay. We didn't think you'd know, we just had to ask. Another point of interest is Mrs Simon's finances. From what we've learned so far, she's a single mother who doesn't work, but she lives in a nice house and drives a relatively decent car. Where does her money come from?'

'When Iain was killed she got enough of a payout from his employers for her to pay off her mortgage. Part of the settlement was that she would collect his pension as long as she lived.'

Campbell gave a slight nod. Chisholm's report on the husband had the bare bones about Iain Simon having died in an industrial accident. While Julie may now be financially secure, she was still left as a widow and single mother.

This again changed the complexion of the case. Julie could have been tortured to give up her bank details. Almost every case he'd ever worked on had boiled down to money, or sex, as a motivator.

'I don't need exact details, but just how big was the payout, and how generous is the pension?'

'Like I said, there was enough of a payout for her to pay off the mortgage. She opted for the pension, so she'd always have an income, rather than a fixed lump sum. I'm not sure about the pension. She never complains about being skint but, on the other hand, she doesn't lead an extravagant life. I've always thought of her as being comfortable with her finances.'

Campbell could feel a frown shaping itself on his forehead. Harper's tone had altered a little when having to repeat himself. The man was irritable and, because of that, he would be more inclined to speak without thinking. He decided it was time to apply a little pressure.

'So, your sister-in-law is financially comfortable, and you believe that your nephew is guilty of dealing drugs. A cynical man would connect those two statements.'

'How dare you insinuate such a thing? Jack may have fallen off the rails but there's no way Julie would be mixed up in it. You might not know this, but her first boyfriend died in her arms after taking a dodgy pill at a party. There's no way she would deal drugs. For me, the fact she hasn't disowned Jack can only be explained as a mother's unconditional love.'

'Please sit back down, Mr Harper.' Campbell kept his tone even – as if they were discussing a trivial matter rather than attempted murder. 'I understand it's an emotive conversation for you, but you must understand that, as detectives, we have to analyse facts, and the facts speak for themselves.'

'DI Campbell is right, Mr Harper.' Lauren picked up the cue of Campbell's toe nudging her ankle. 'We have to be cold and analyse the facts for what they tell us. It's our job to amass enough information so that we can find out who did this horrible thing to your sister-in-law.'

Harper flopped into his chair. 'I'm sorry. I shouldn't have snapped at you like that. What with looking after my wife and poor Gracie last night, I hardly got a wink of sleep.'

'That's okay. We understand that it's all very personal for you.' Lauren sat back in her chair, folded one leg over the other, and smoothed her skirt. 'We're just trying to eliminate all possible suspects. Can I be honest with you?'

'Of course.'

Campbell noticed the way Harper was looking at Lauren. There was a trace of lust and a complete lack of fear. If the man's wife wasn't so high on his meagre list of suspects, he'd pity him for the trap he was running into.

'In cases like this, there are just three reasons why someone would launch such an attack. The first is money, the second is sex and the third is retribution. That's what we're taught. It's in all the handbooks, but, can I tell you something?' She didn't give him a chance to answer. 'Retribution can, almost always, be traced back to being for sexual or monetary reasons.'

Harper gave a nervous laugh. 'So you're saying she was almost killed because of money or sex? Don't look at me, I'm married to her sister and this business keeps a very good roof over our heads.'

'What makes you think we're looking at you, Mr Harper?'

Campbell watched as Lauren stood and leaned her hands on a sideboard to get a closer look at a framed brochure on the wall behind Harper. The graphic designer was running his eyes over Lauren's figure, making sure he got a good look at every part of her body.

'Well, you're here aren't you?' Harper's attempt at a smile travelled dangerously close to becoming a leer.

Lauren turned to face him. 'We're here because we need your inside knowledge. It doesn't seem like money is the reason so we need to know if she was seeing anyone. You do understand that anyone she was seeing is a potential suspect for us? If this person was married, or in a serious relationship, their partner would become a suspect.'

'I'm sure my wife is a better person to ask about Julie's love life. They're sisters after all, and sisters talk don't they?'

'DI Campbell used his mobile to take a snap of Julie in one of the pictures she has hanging in the hall. It's something we always do – being able to see the victim's face is a great motivator for us. When DC Bhaki saw the picture last night, he almost choked on his cuppa. He says that Mrs Simon and your wife could pass as twins – despite your wife being two years older.'

A patronising expression took over Harper's face. 'Well, they are sisters.'

'Would you say that your wife is a beautiful woman, Mr Harper?'

'Of course.' The answer came without hesitation.

'Then you must think that Julie is as well. I certainly hope I look that good when I get to her age.'

'Yes, she's a good-looking woman. What of it? I married a beautiful woman. It's not a crime for her sister to be beautiful as well is it?'

'Of course it isn't.' Lauren bent at the waist to scratch her knee. 'I just wondered if you'd ever been attracted to her?'

'Oh bloody hell, what is this? Yes, I fancied my wife's sister. No, I've never slept with her. I've also fancied Angelina Jolie, but it doesn't mean I'm responsible for her and Brad Pitt separating.'

'Mr Harper.' Campbell made sure there was a certain amount of steel in his voice. 'I'd like to remind you that you are talking to a police officer. DC Phillips is merely asking a pertinent question. Were you sleeping with Julie Simon?'

'No. Absolutely not.' Harper was on his feet again; hands planted on the desk. 'If my Wendy knew you were harassing me, instead of trying to catch whoever stabbed her sister, she'd be making complaints to every one of your superiors.'

Campbell was about to fire a response at Harper when he felt Lauren's hand on his arm. 'Leave it, sir. Julie's phone records will tell us whether or not Mr Harper has been slipping across town to sample a younger version of what he's got at home.'

Campbell was a pace away from the door when he heard a single damning word.

'Wait.'

Chapter 10

The corridors of A&E looked just the same in daylight as they had last night. At ten in the morning, there may be less demand on the staff than at kicking out time on a Friday or Saturday, but there was still a fair amount of industrious activity. Porters moved patients around, while cleaners scrubbed various areas down. The smell of their antiseptic chemicals filled Bhaki's nose.

To make sure his visit wasn't a waste of time, he'd called ahead. The secretary he'd spoken to couldn't guarantee a specific time, but she'd implied that barring emergencies, the surgeon should be free between ten and half past.

He asked a nurse where he could find Dr Higgs and made his way to the correct office.

The door was open and, when the surgeon looked up from her desk, he was waved in. He took a seat, and looked around at various files and medical textbooks on the shelf, while the surgeon continued her call.

Several different mugs adorning the cluttered shelf told him the office was used by more than just Dr Higgs. A framed photo on the wall showed a group of doctors and nurses at the bedside of a child who had both thumbs raised and a huge smile. In the centre of the picture stood Janet Evans. Her smile every bit as broad as the child's.

He got why the picture was there. It was one of their success stories and would be used to inspire them on their darker days. In the same way the team used pictures of victims to spur them on, the successes of the A&E department would be ones to treasure as their failures would be raw and visceral.

Bhaki had dealt with enough distraught relatives to have experienced the whole gamut of emotions. Broken-hearted people were wont to rage against injustices, point fingers of blame and fall apart in a variety of heart-rending ways.

It wouldn't matter to the bereaved that the doctors felt guilt at not being able to save a life; that they wouldn't be able to sleep as they questioned their every action – wondering if there was something they could have done differently to save a patient.

The surgeon ended her call and looked up at Bhaki with tired eyes. 'Morning. I'm not sure I can add much to what I told you last night.'

'Thanks for seeing me, Dr Higgs. I only have a few questions and will try not to take up too much of your time.'

'Ask away. I'm yours until they need me elsewhere. Could be a minute; could be hours. And you can call me Dr Becca – everyone else does.'

Bhaki understood the unspoken message and got straight to the point. 'The wound you told me about last night, have you had any further thoughts on what could have caused it?'

'I've thought about it a lot but haven't got any ideas. My best guess is that it was caused by something blunt and smooth.'

Bhaki struggled to keep the blush from his face. 'If I was to suggest a dildo to you, would it fit with the tearing?'

'It's not impossible.' Her face clouded in thought. 'That's really twisted, and it doesn't explain the scratches.'

'What scratches?'

'Sorry, I meant to tell you last night but didn't get chance. There were faint scratches on her stomach wall.'

Bhaki pulled a face and regretted it when he saw her frown. 'Wouldn't they be caused by the knife?'

'Not at all. They were ragged scrapes rather than defined cuts. You know the kind of scrape you get when you fall and put your hand out? They're the kind of scratches I found.'

'How many were there, and what do you think caused them?'

'I counted three and couldn't begin to guess what caused them.'

'Can you at least give me your best guess?'

'Something hard. Either metallic or a stiff plastic.'

'What about the shape of this mysterious object, could you guess at what it was like? What size it was?'

'All I can say for sure is that it would have at least one ragged edge.' A finger pointed to her own belly. 'Believe it or not, the human stomach isn't actually very big. The scratches on her stomach wall were no more than a half inch in length; therefore, whatever caused them wasn't huge – or at least its abrasive part wasn't.'

'How does the wound compare with other stab wounds you've seen?'

'It's very precise. Almost surgical. Most of the knife wounds we see are ragged affairs where someone has lashed out in anger. This one was clinical.' Dr Becca pulled a textbook from the shelf, found the page she wanted, and showed it to Bhaki. There was a diagram of the human body. 'The stomach is located here, behind the lower ribs, whoever stabbed Mrs Simon, managed to miss the lower intestines. They also showed enough restraint to not go right through the stomach. If they had, they could have severed the aorta or vena cava. The spleen is in that same area and they've missed that too.'

'Wow. Sounds like she's been very lucky?'

Dr Becca nodded. 'She has. It's a miracle she didn't die from the wound, or the infection she's picked up from having her stomach cut open.'

'Really?' Bhaki's thoughts returned to his earlier theory of the victim being on the table when she was stabbed. 'Is it possible that the victim was on her feet when this happened?'

'It is.' A confused expression twisted her face. 'But it's highly unlikely. There would be an awful lot of pain and the wound would be different. In most stabbings, the victim recoils, or moves, while the knife is still inside them. This leads to secondary cuts when the knife is being withdrawn.'

'You mean like an exit wound?'

'I do. But there wasn't any sign of that. Mrs Simon would have been in a lot of pain. She would have screamed, and her body would have moved as a reaction to the trauma of the wound. It doesn't look like that happened, so I'd assume she was either drugged or bound to keep her still.' The textbook was put back on the shelf. 'We took some of her blood from the wound, so we can test it. I'll let you know if we find out she was drugged.'

Bhaki felt his excitement growing, as his earlier suspicions were proving correct. 'I take it that a kitchen table would work as a makeshift operating table?'

'It would. If she wasn't drugged it's possible she was tied to it.'

'Did you see any marks on her wrists?' Bhaki was hoping ligatures, left by cable ties, would be present to confirm his theory.

'Not that I saw, but in fairness, I was concentrating on her stomach. Once she was stabilised, a nurse cleaned her down.'

'Is there anything else you can tell me?'

'Just that I called ICU to see how she is. She's developed peritonitis, but that's not unusual with such a deep cut. They're pumping her full of antibiotics and keeping her sedated. I know it's not the news you want to hear, but I reckon it'll be at least a couple of days before her medication can be reduced enough for her to be able to speak to you. That's providing she pulls through.'

Bhaki thanked Dr Becca and left feeling more confused than when he'd arrived. The scratches on Julie's stomach made her stabbing even more puzzling.

Chapter 11

Campbell peered through the windscreen as he pulled out of the junction. Yesterday's drizzle had evolved into a series of torrential showers. The car's wipers were struggling to maintain visibility – despite being on their highest setting – while the air-conditioning was fighting a losing battle against the mist forming on the inside of its windows.

'What do you make of Harper then, do you think his wife is the one who attacked her sister?'

'It seems a bit of a stretch to me. So, he got a blowjob five years ago when she was away with friends – if it had happened recently I'd think more of it.'

'You're right, to a point.' Campbell turned onto Dalston Road and pulled up behind a bus. 'Except that there's no such thing as a statute of limitations on anger and revenge. Perhaps the wait is her serving her revenge cold. Perhaps she's smart enough to wait so that she's removed from suspicion.'

'I think you're wrong. Think about it; Harper would have been ejected years ago if that was the case. According to DS Chisholm, Mrs Harper is a solicitor. She could divorce him with ease. There's no way she's waited five years to get her revenge. That's five years of sharing a bed, living with a secret eating away at the relationship. Tell me, do you think your wife would carry on as normal for five years if she knew about the night you spent in my bed?'

Campbell knew the answer to that question – Sarah wouldn't wait five years to get her revenge. He'd be lucky if she waited five seconds.

The night he'd spent with Lauren was one filled with regret for him. Not only had he cheated on his wife – days after his son was born; Evans had found out and had used the information to blackmail his way in to a consultancy role. He now spent half his mental energy worrying he'd lose his wife and son because of an encounter he couldn't even remember having. He'd been pissed up and his memory of the evening was sketchy at best. One minute he'd been in a crowded bar and the next he was waking up in Lauren's bed. What had happened between those memories was a mystery, but he'd been naked when he woke, and Lauren had led him to believe they'd had sex.

'You have a point. She'd kick my arse out the door before I could even say I was sorry.'

'Exactly. I think it's a one-off and they've managed to keep the secret. We should ask her about her sister's love life but should steer well clear of mentioning her husband. There's nothing to be gained by hastening the end of their marriage.'

'What do you mean? Do you know something about their marriage that I don't?'

'Did you see the way Harper was looking at me? He's a player, and there's no doubt in my mind he'll cheat on his wife at any given opportunity. It's only a matter of time before she catches him in the wrong bed.'

Campbell didn't know how to answer that statement, so he didn't even try. Her assessment of Martin Harper could well be the same one she had of him. It wasn't a good basis for a professional relationship. He was supposed to earn her respect. Waking up in her bed with no memory of the evening before had been the worst possible start.

'It's hardly a surprise he was looking at you – the way you were exhibiting yourself.' He decided attack was the best way to mount a defence. 'You dress as if you're out on the pull rather than working as a police officer.'

'With all due respect, *sir*, I've caught you ogling me many a time, so I think you complaining about the clothes I choose to wear is hypocritical. You're not so quick to criticise when you're the one looking down my blouse. Tell me, when a suspect is looking at me and getting distracted, is my dress sense a problem then?' Lauren pulled a compact from her bag. 'I dress the way I do because I like the attention. If the team gets a result, because some sad wanker would rather try and see my tits or leer over my legs than think straight, I figure it's a bonus. I suggest you take a good look in the mirror, *sir*. Until you can stop your own leching, you haven't got a leg to stand on.'

Campbell bit down on his response and chewed at the inside of his mouth. He'd just made an awkward situation a whole lot worse. His only recourse was to hide behind his rank, but that would mask the problem rather than solve it. Going forward, he knew he'd have to start over with Lauren; prove himself anew by keeping his eyes where they should be.

What rankled him most of all was, that as she was calling him out, she'd never once raised her voice or shown any sign of anger. Her rant had been delivered in a calm fashion which made it all the more effective.

Chapter 12

The trip into town had done Evans both good and harm. His aching muscles had resented every step, but he'd enjoyed seeing a couple of familiar faces and had managed to source a dozen or so crime novels, for a pound or two apiece, in the various charity shops he'd visited.

As he always did when he was in town with time on his hands, he'd spent an hour looking around Waterstones and chatting with the manager. The young hipster looked nothing like a dedicated reader until you noticed the words 'BOOK WORM' tattooed across his knuckles. The conversation had borne fruit for Evans, as he now knew of three book launches he fancied attending.

It had been good to enjoy a pint at the Kings Head, and eat a meal that wasn't microwaved or delivered in a box.

Better still had been the chance to interact with members of the public again. To see the centre of town and overhear a dozen conversations he had no business listening to. Carlisle and its people were in his blood, and he loved that he'd dedicated his career to making the border city a safer place for them to live.

He turned the corner, into the car park of the apartment block, and saw a familiar car.

Maureen Leighton's Bentley was parked in his usual spot. As ever, the back window was open to allow her cigarette smoke an escape route.

This was the first time she'd appeared at his home, and he was a little disconcerted she knew where he lived. She wasn't a problem herself, but her knuckle-headed brothers could be. While they were just about smart enough to know they'd never win a fair fight with him, a surprise attack or ambush would be just the kind of thing they'd love to do.

The car window raised with a faint purr. The door swung open and a woman emerged. As ever, Maureen Leighton was dressed in a velour tracksuit.

Her right hand clutched a packet of cigarettes and a mobile phone, while her left held the kind of tall, narrow bag used when bottles of spirits or wine were given as gifts.

'Hey, Harry.' The gift bag was extended towards him. 'Got a wee something for you.'

Evans' blood chilled a little. Maureen Leighton was head of the family behind most of Cumbria's organised crime.

Over the years they'd struck up a kind of cordial relationship based on mutual respect. While it may go against the grain for a copper and a criminal to have a friendship of sorts, Evans knew there were far worse criminals than the Leightons. They dealt in the smaller things and kept rival firms from encroaching on their territory. Sure, they may well dish out a beating or two, but their retribution was usually aimed at the criminal classes. These assaults may break laws, but the victims never asked for the police.

What didn't sit well with him was her giving him a gift, in the middle of a car park, in broad daylight. It only took the wrong person to be driving by and he'd face all kinds of accusations ...

He pointed to the door. 'With me.'

Once she was in his ground floor apartment, he whirled to face her as Tripod nosed his legs in greeting. 'What the fuck are you trying to do to me, shouting that across a bloody car park?'

'That's no way to greet an old friend.' She gave a lazy, unconcerned shrug. 'You think someone's going to be bothered about me giving you a present? You're retired now.'

'And you run most of the crime in this county.' Evans scowled and leaned against a wall. 'Now you're showing up here with something that can be construed as a bribe. If anyone who knows us both had seen that, they'd start thinking I was on the take.'

Maureen flapped a hand. 'You worry too much. Get a couple of glasses and have a drop of this. It's a twenty-five-year-old Speyside.'

'Are you being an imbecile on purpose? If they think I'm in your pocket, do you know what they'll do?'

'They'll look into your finances, see you're clean and then leave you alone.'

'Wrong. They'll do that, and they'll also look at every case I was ever involved in where the name Leighton came up. Trust me, that's a lot of cases.' He paused his rant to glower at her. 'You might have been smart enough to keep you and your brothers out of jail all these years, but don't think we don't know everything you're up to.'

'I doubt that. If you did you'd have nicked us years ago.'

'Just how many stupid pills have you taken today? You've been allowed to remain in place because you're not that bad. You keep a grip on things and, apart from the odd dickhead getting a kicking, you're pretty much peaceful. If we took you down, whoever took your place would invariably be more trouble than you are. Plus, there would almost certainly be a gang war between whichever firms decided to step into your shoes.'

Maureen's face dropped all its joviality as Evans outlined the hard truths. He wasn't telling her to be cruel, but she needed to know where she stood.

'So, Maureen, why are you here?'

'Can't I drop by to see an old friend who's been on the receiving end of a good kicking?'

'You're a week late.' Evans wasn't prepared to listen to her excuses. There was no way she was visiting him without some ulterior motive. 'Want to get to the real reason for your visit?'

She withdrew the whisky from the bottle bag. 'Get some glasses will you?'

Evans got two crystal glasses from the kitchen cupboard – as far as he was concerned, malt whisky deserved nothing less – and carried them into the living room with Maureen trailing behind him.

She took a look round the room and gave a low whistle. He knew she was looking at his book collection. Some people decorated a feature wall with patterned wallpaper; he had floor to ceiling bookshelves.

'I knew you liked reading but never expected you liked it this much.'

Evans shrugged at her. 'Your point, Maureen? You didn't come here with an expensive bottle of whisky just because I got a kicking.'

'You're right, I didn't. I came here because you walked into one of our pubs, picked a fight with the biggest guy in there and did nothing to defend yourself when he started throwing punches.'

He hadn't known the pub was owned by the Leightons. Not that it mattered whose name was on the title deeds. It had been the nearest place he could find where he was guaranteed to find help with his bout of self-flagellation.

What he didn't want her knowing, was the reason why he'd done what he did. In all the years he'd spent breaking rules it was the line he'd crossed the furthest, and if Maureen got wind of it she'd use it against him.

'Let's just say that I was feeling a little drunk and more than a little pissed off. In case you weren't aware, it was the same day the trial ended.' Evans took a sip of his whisky and savoured the smooth burn it left on his throat. 'I went in there looking for a fight – that I don't deny. As soon as I'd picked it though, I knew it was a mistake. Knew it was unfair for me to walk in, pick a fight and then knock seven bells out of someone.'

'Are you telling me you took that kicking rather than defend yourself?' Her eyes narrowed. 'You're lying, Harry, and not just to me but to yourself as well. The reason you changed your mind wasn't because it wasn't fair on the other guy. You changed your mind because you were afraid you'd go too far once you got started. I'm right aren't I?'

Evans took another drink of his whisky rather than answer her. There was a certain amount of truth to her words; had he balled a fist that night, there was every chance he would have used it far too much. The fight would have become a savage beating. Unless he'd been restrained by bystanders or arrested, he may well have kept punching long after his opponent had stopped being able to defend himself.

In his own way, he was happy for her to think he possessed such a streak. Not only did it hide his true reasons for picking the fight, it would make her keep a tighter leash on her brothers. Tony and Dennis both had more muscle than brain. Due to this disparity, they had a tendency to hit first and think later. If at all.

As Maureen crossed one pink velour-clad leg over the other, she held up her cigarette packet and lifted an eyebrow.

'Sure.' He waved her permission to light up and fished his own cigarettes from his shirt pocket.

Tired of being on the back foot in the conversation, he decided to take control with a few questions of his own. Bhaki had snuck in a quick call and updated him on their progress – or lack thereof. With nothing better to do with his time, he might as well try to help – even if he was being kept on the sideline.

'Jack Simon sends his regards.'

'Who?' There was no artifice to her answer. No deception on her face, just puzzlement. 'Who's Jack Simon and why would he be sending me his regards?'

'A schoolboy who got caught with enough drugs to earn himself a "with intent to supply" charge. He's currently at Deerbolt.'

A wicked phlegm-filled cackle erupted from her mouth. 'Goodness sake, Harry, you know I'd never have anything to do with dealing to kids.' A nonchalant shrug. 'Can't say about those who buy goods from me, but I can tell you there's no way I, or anyone who works for me, sells that shit to kids. You said yoursel', we're allowed to go about our business because you know there's worse than us out there.'

It had been a longshot at best, but it was also a way to re-establish his dominance.

'You're right. I didn't think it was you, but I had to ask.'

'Perhaps you did. What interests me now is who this Jack Simon is. Care to tell me?'

Evans ground out his cigarette and drained the last of his whisky. 'Not really. If you don't know him, the reasons for me asking aren't important.'

'Like hell they aren't. You've never done anything you don't feel important. You just don't want to tell me. Which means it's to do with a case. You may have been officially retired, but I bet your team still come to you looking for answers and insights.' Her eyes clouded over and drifted unseeing around the room as she lost herself in thought. The click of her fingers came without any warning. 'There was a woman got herself stabbed. I saw it on Border Crack and Deekabout. Her surname was Simon. Would I be right in guessing it's her lad who's in Deerbolt?'

Evans gave an exaggerated nod. Like everyone else in their age bracket, Border TV's News and Lookaround was a staple part of their early evening. Maureen joining the dots wasn't a surprise to him. She may dress like a seventies cushion and smoke like a chimney on bonus, but she possessed a sharp mind and cunning intelligence.

She lit another cigarette. 'You asking me about the boy is your way of finding out if I had anything to do with the mother's stabbing, or if I know whose hand may have held the knife.'

'Well, do you?' Evans kept his tone mild to match hers. As ever with their verbal sparring, they both showed the other respect by having a conversation rather than a shouting match.

'I don't.' A plume of smoke travelled across the room. 'And we both know that if I did know, it would depend upon the name as to whether or not I told you.'

While Evans knew Maureen was an accomplished liar, he couldn't see any trace of deception – either in her face or body language. Strange as it seemed, he believed her and told her as much.

It just seemed odd to him that the mother of someone doing time for dealing had been stabbed and had something pushed into the wound.

Evans was pouring a second whisky when he realised they'd been looking at the stabbing all wrong. The, almost surgical, care of the cut was a clue they'd overlooked. As were the tearing of the stomach wall, and scratches inside Julie's stomach. All of their theories were based on the assumption that Julie had something inserted into her when they should have been asking what might have been taken out.

He couldn't speak to any of the team while Maureen was here, so he directed the conversation towards who else could have supplied Jack Simon with the drugs. Either he'd get a name from her, or she'd tire of his fishing and leave.

Chapter 13

Even with all of the team in the room, there was little noise as they each filed their reports and waited for DI Campbell to begin the meeting he'd called.

Bhaki could tell from the expressions on Lauren and Chisholm's faces that they'd both had differing results. Lauren's mouth was twisted in frustration, while Chisholm's face wore the look of someone who knew a piece of gossip that fell just short of qualifying as juicy.

'Right then.' Campbell walked over to the whiteboard they used to outline all their case details. 'Martin Harper had, what Bill Clinton denied as, "sexual relations" with Julie Simon. But it happened five years ago and he says it's very unlikely his wife found out about it. Other than that, we've got the square root of sod all to go on. Forensics have come back and said they found a lot of smudged prints on all the obvious places, like door handles and light switches. I would hope I don't need to explain to anyone that smudges are synonymous with someone wearing gloves.'

Bhaki shook his head at the DI's suggestion. 'I take it you didn't get them to give the house a more thorough sweep?'

'No. Not with the budget we've got.'

There, in a nutshell, was the difference between Evans and Campbell. The latter worried about budgets, while Evans did what he had to do then dealt with the fallout when DCI Grantham found out how much he'd spent.

As exhilarating as Evans' methods were, Bhaki knew they couldn't be allowed to continue. It was a miracle he'd got away with his behaviour for as long as he had. Campbell's ways were straight from the handbook and echoed all the training he'd undergone. Times were changing and he'd have to get used to doing everything by the book again.

'There is one spot of interesting news, sir.'

'What is it, Neil? What have you got?' Campbell's voice echoed the mild excitement in Chisholm's.

'I finally managed to get Julie's phone out of the evidence store. She was meeting people on Tinder. Every month until her son got put in Deerbolt she'd arrange a meeting. I'm still working on the details, but I should be able to get names, times and dates for you.'

Ideas whirled round Bhaki's mind as they all chipped in with questions. Back and forth they went, pushing and probing at the information Chisholm had and the things they wanted to know.

When they all ran out of steam, it was determined that Bhaki should go and see Wendy. Ask if she knew about Julie's Tinder encounters.

Lauren and Campbell would run the names of Julie's paramours through the database to see if any were known to the police. Then they'd start interviewing these men. Chisholm, as ever, would be left to run the office and liaise with everyone.

A muted beep in his pocket made him pull his phone out.

Chapter 14

Bhaki took a seat in the minimalist lounge and tossed a smile Gracie's way. Her eyes were red and puffy – as were her aunt's. Wendy shared a sofa with her niece and had a protective arm draped across the girl's shoulders.

After reading Evans' theory, he'd done as his old boss had instructed and shared it with the team. He hadn't wanted to take any credit, but Evans had been insistent in his usual sweary way.

Campbell had been specific with the questions he wanted answers to. He was to find out if Julie had taken any trips abroad or if they'd holidayed anywhere. Evans' theory that the mother was a drug mule, with her stomach full of narcotic-filled condoms, wasn't one he was convinced of, but he'd learned not to question his former DI's hunches.

For him, it just didn't add up. The boy had been caught with cannabis and ecstasy tablets, not heroin or cocaine. There was no need to import ecstasy or cannabis when there was more than enough produced in the UK.

The only way he could see it making any sense, was for Julie to have been intent on setting up her own network and establishing herself as a dealer and importer. Even if she were, he couldn't see the need. She had the income from her husband's pension and there was the girl to consider.

While he'd been a copper long enough to know that there are elements of society that show neither care nor love for their offspring, he didn't believe Gracie was unloved by her mother. She had been too upset, and everything he'd heard from the aunt and uncle spoke of a loving, tightly-knit family.

He smiled again. 'Gracie, where did you and your mum go on holiday last year?'

'We stayed with Grandma and Grandad for a couple of weeks in the summer.' The girl sat up straight while answering his question. 'They live near Blackpool. We went to the Pleasure Beach and up the tower. We even went to the Tower Ballroom. Mum danced around like she was on *Strictly*.' A roll of the eyes. 'It was sooo embarrassing.'

'And where are you going this year?'

Chapter 17

Ally Longridge hadn't been what Campbell was expecting. His preconceptions had led him to think that guys who used Tinder were at the lower end of the dating scale. They'd have little going for them visually, and would use the site to pinpoint women whose lack of confidence or looks, meant desperate measures were necessary.

Sitting behind his desk in an accountant's office, Longridge was a handsome, well-groomed man who exuded charm and charisma in spades. The problem Campbell had, was that it was nothing more than a front. His eyes would flit around the room before returning to their destination of choice.

As was her way, Lauren was displaying an indifferent nonchalance to his examination of her cleavage, but Campbell noticed a minute stiffening of her shoulders and there was a slight falseness to her tone. She was leading with the questions but he was ready to jump in whenever he felt it necessary.

'Thanks for seeing us at such short notice, Mr Longridge.'

'I'm always happy to help the police, my dear. Especially when they are as well presented as yourself. I thought female cops were all sensible shoes and a butch front to prove they are as good as any man. I can see that I'm quite clearly wrong.'

That one sentence about female cops explained to Campbell just why such an outwardly attractive man needed to use Tinder to get laid.

To him, Lauren's giggle was an obvious fake, but Longridge's smile never faltered.

'Mr Longridge, you flatter me. We just need to ask you a few questions and then we'll let you get on with your work. I'm sure it's very important.'

'My work is important but less so than assisting the police. How may I help you?'

'First of all, I should let you know that we're investigating a serious assault that may yet become a murder. You're known to have met with the victim after hooking up on Tinder. We'd like to know your whereabouts yesterday afternoon.'

The way Longridge sat back in his chair with an easy smile, told Campbell the man had a strong alibi. 'I was in a meeting with a client and our managing director. It started at one and finished at five.' A manicured hand reached out and pressed a button on the phone on his desk. 'Melanie, can you come in for a moment please?'

The office door opened and a stunning redhead walked in. 'Yes, Mr Longridge?'

'Can you tell these police officers where I was yesterday afternoon?'

Melanie shot him a look of disgust which bounced off unnoticed. 'He was in a meeting with Mr Nolan and one of our clients.' She started towards the door. 'Would you like me to get the minutes?'

'No, it's fine, thank you.'

As much as Campbell would have liked Longridge to have been guilty, the meeting provided him with an alibi. There was no doubt in his mind the man was a blatant lech. He was equally sure Melanie despised her boss and his wandering eyes.

Longridge was the type to have hired Melanie on looks alone. Campbell guessed her work life would be spent awaiting his next inappropriate comment or perverted leer. With luck, the accountant would go too far and she'd file a complaint which would cost him his job.

As they walked back to the car he checked his mobile. Just as he'd hoped, there was an email from Chisholm. A third name was most welcome after drawing two blanks.

Their first interview had stopped as soon as Lauren had seen Craig Adamson. She'd been discreet and waited until they were in the car, but had told him that Adamson was well known for his bed-hopping exploits. From what she'd said about the man, Campbell got the impression Lauren had slept with him at some point.

Adamson was a builder and was six and a half feet of muscle and hormones. If he'd stuck his sausage-like fingers into Julie Simon to retrieve anything, the hole in her stomach would have been far bigger.

The third name was the most promising so far, and he felt a pulse of excitement that he may be about to confront the man who'd stabbed Julie Simon.

Chapter 18

The sheet of numbers made perfect sense to Bhaki as he ran a finger down the various columns. Try as he might, he couldn't find anything which piqued either suspicion or interest.

Julie Simon's finances were in order and there were explanations for everything he was looking at. Regular amounts were spent at the supermarket, or on Amazon. There was the odd peak in her spending which could be explained by one of the kids' birthdays, or a short break, but there was nothing which suggested she was involved in anything illegal.

He'd worked out that Julie's husband's pension was worth just under thirty-thousand pounds a year, and that she managed to save ten grand of that in a separate account. His best guess was that when the time came, those savings would be used to put the children through university or help them get on the property ladder.

His interest was piqued when he saw it was Julie who'd paid for the hotel rooms when she'd arranged a meeting. She'd taken all the right measures to protect her safety and privacy, and he admired her for it.

A thought niggled at him so he put the bank and credit card statements face down on his desk, and leaned back in his chair to look at the ceiling.

Julie Simon's money could be traced from the point of entry into her bank until she either spent or saved it. The withdrawals she made from cash machines were too small to be anything more than her making sure she had a few quid in her purse for the kids or a pint of milk.

On the other hand, her son was caught with enough drugs for an "intent to supply" charge to stick. There's no way he could have been involved in dealing drugs without making a sizeable amount of money.

Had Jack been caught on his first attempt at dealing, it would mean he'd either purchased the drugs in advance, or he still owed for them.

Bhaki knew he needed to look into the boy's case to determine the quantity and value of the drugs. He'd also need to check the boy's finances to see if he had a savings account he'd withdrawn money from.

If Jack had been dealing for a while, he would have had the money to show for it. Even the stupidest of suppliers knew better than to stiff their dealers. It was a quick way to lose allegiances. Loyalty was a fragile thing in the criminal world, and those who supplied dealers tended to keep themselves hidden through fear. Had Jack been mistreated by his supplier, or aggrieved at his payment, he'd have been more inclined to offer up some names when arrested. That hadn't happened; which meant either he still owed for the drugs he was caught with, or he was more frightened of the threats laid down by his supplier than he was of going into a young offenders institution.

Bhaki used his computer to find the necessary details and printed them off. He planned to call the arresting officer for more background and then if he still felt there was something amiss after reading the files, he'd go and see Evans. If anyone could make sense of the hare-brained idea his mind was cultivating, it was his former guv.

He was in luck. His call was answered and the officer he spoke to could remember the case. While the woman was friendly enough to him, she was insistent her report featured any suspicions she may have had.

The first report he read was a statement from the boy's head of year. Jack Simon had been a well-behaved pupil with average grades. His school attendance was good and he was not someone the head of year had expected to be involved with drugs. The report went on to describe Jack as socially awkward. While not an outcast, he floated in the wilderness between the cool kids and the nerds, with just one friend for company.

Bhaki read the transcript from the boy's interview. Jack had answered every question put to him and had been insistent throughout the interview that he'd been framed.

The arresting officer's notes were concise and to the point. She'd accepted the word of the head of year, and the janitor who'd opened Jack's school locker after receiving an anonymous tip-off. She'd pointed out that his story of being set up had carried a ring of truth – especially with the way he'd been caught. Bhaki read every letter and punctuation mark but couldn't find any mention of an investigation into where the boy had got the money to buy the drugs he was found with, or where he'd stashed the money already made from previous sales. Jack's refusal to point a finger towards whoever he suspected had planted the drugs, had gone against him.

In Bhaki's mind, the head of year's statement supported the boy's claim that he'd been set up. In his experience, dealers weren't social outcasts – they were the people who addicts would seek out for their next fix. They'd always have company.

This line of thought was backed up even further by the statement from Jack's sole friend. The friend defended him like a brother and swore there was no way Jack was selling drugs to anyone. He'd told of conversations about music, football, and girls they fancied but didn't dare ask out.

Bhaki remembered his own schooldays, as one of only four brown faces in a schoolyard. He'd fit in, to a point, but was never accepted into the upper echelons inhabited by the kids who excelled at sports, and could boast the more fashionable clothes or exotic holidays. Life on the fringes had been passable and he'd been lucky to only have to deal with a few incidents of racial abuse. Most of all though, he could recall his desperation to be accepted by those he wanted to emulate – how far he'd been prepared to go to impress the kind of people he was now paid to protect or imprison, depending upon their life choices.

There was a picture of Jack Simon in the file. It showed a scared boy with a wisp of dark hair on his top lip that was trying to be a moustache. He was good-looking enough and had fewer spots than the average teenager, but it was the fear in his eyes that Bhaki knew he would remember. Whether the fear was of retribution from his supplier or the fact he'd be spending time in a young offenders institution didn't matter. The boy's life was about to undergo a drastic change, and it showed that he knew it would be years before he could recover his life after the experience.

Chapter 19

The man looking back at him, across the table, didn't look as nervous as Campbell felt he should. Dr Stephen Wood had been rounded up by a couple of woodentops and brought to the station for his interview.

He'd been one of Julie's Tinder dates, and as soon as Campbell had learned the man was a GP, Wood had received a promotion to the top of his suspect list.

Campbell was banking that the more formal setting of an interview room, and the fact he'd had the doctor cautioned, would loosen his tongue.

'So, Dr Wood, you say you were at home, sick, yesterday afternoon.'

'That's right.' Wood's voice was even, and his body was still. 'I picked up a bug at the weekend and didn't think my patients would appreciate me spreading it to them when they were already ill. I took an extra day off to make sure I was in good health for my return today. I took the advice I'd give to my patients and went for a walk to get some fresh air and exercise.'

Lauren spoke for the first time. 'Where did you go for your walk?'

'Along Cumwhinton Road and down towards the Garlands before I looped back. It's a walk I often take with my wife.'

Campbell noted there was no hesitation in the doctor's answer or signs of any raised stress levels.

'That would put you in the vicinity of Parkfield Close, wouldn't it?'

'Is that part of the housing estate there? If it is, then I guess my walk would have taken me that way.'

Lauren's knowledge of Carlisle's streets was something Campbell had yet to learn. Unless the doctor had mentioned Parkfield Close himself, he'd never have connected the names without looking at a street map. He'd memorised the various areas and had learned the major roads around the border city but had yet to learn the individual streets.

To Campbell, Lauren's smile was that of a bloodhound picking up a new scent. She was homing in on Wood, and it was only a matter of time before she started asking questions that would be increasingly difficult to answer.

'What time did you go for your walk?'

'Back of three. I wanted to get home in time to put tea on for my wife. May I ask why you're asking me these questions, and why you had me cautioned when I would have been happy to come in and answer them?'

His tone was too calm for Campbell's liking. Wood displayed no signs of stress – his movements were slow and deliberate which made him suspect the doctor would be skilled with a needle, scalpel or kitchen knife if the need arose.

Lauren's tone was devoid of any flirtatiousness or respect when she answered the doctor's questions.

'You were brought in, under caution, because a woman you met through Tinder was brutally attacked in her home on Parkfield Close yesterday afternoon. She's now in ICU at the infirmary, fighting for her life. Since we started conducting this interview you have admitted to being in the vicinity of her home at the time she was attacked.'

Campbell was watching for Wood's reaction and, other than a flash of horror, there wasn't one.

'I'm sorry to hear that. I do hope she makes a full recovery.' He turned to Campbell with an all-boys-together look. 'I have met a number of women through Tinder; could you be so kind as to tell me which one has been attacked?'

'The victim's name is Julie Simon. You met with her nine months ago.'

Wood's eyes went blank as he scrolled his memory. 'Ah yes, I remember her. A lovely lady. I didn't know she lived in Carlisle though. As I remember it, we met at the Premier Inn.'

'Her wound was a precise one.' Lauren put her elbows on the table and leaned close to the doctor. 'It went up under her ribs and into her stomach. There was also tearing of her stomach wall and internal scratching. The surgeon who saved her life told us most stab wounds are rough and ready with slashes. We believe she wasn't so much stabbed, as operated on.' She raised a hand. 'Before you ask, we think she swallowed an item that someone wanted and then they operated on her to get it. So, what we'd like to know, Dr Wood, is what did you take from Julie Simon's stomach yesterday afternoon?'

'Nothing. I didn't see, speak to, or operate on her. I went for a walk, that's all. I'm sorry, but you're asking the wrong man.'

Campbell had expected to see a foot or hand move with the increased stress of Lauren's probing, but Wood still exuded an air of confidence. It was time to shake him a little further.

'You seem very calm about our questions. That tells me either you're innocent, or you've rehearsed all this in your head long before it came to be.' Campbell slammed the palm of his hand onto the table. 'Which is it, Doc? You fit the profile of someone who'd be able to operate on her. You're a married man carrying on behind his wife's back. Tell us, Doc, what was so important to you that you had to cut it out of her stomach?'

'You're wrong, detective. I didn't do it. And I'm not carrying on behind my wife's back. We have an open relationship. Both of us see other people.'

'Do you expect me to believe that?'

'Believe what you will. I might not have an alibi but I had my phone with me, and if you triangulate the signals for my whereabouts yesterday you'll see I didn't go within a hundred yards of Parkfield Close.' Wood pulled his mobile from his shirt pocket and laid it on the table. 'If you'd care to look at the message logs, you'll see I was in regular contact with a lady I'm hoping to meet this weekend. We were messaging each other every couple of minutes. There wasn't time for me to go around cutting things out of people's stomachs between messages.'

Lauren's hand got to the phone first, and after a few seconds of fiddling she nodded at Wood and slid it back across the table.

Campbell apologised to Wood and hoped his frustration at hitting another dead end hadn't crept into his voice.

Chapter 20

Evans had to ease his pace so Tripod could keep up. There was no need to hurry:

Bhaki wouldn't get to the apartment for at least another half hour but, like a kid on Christmas Eve who wanted to go to bed early, he felt the sooner he was ready for the young detective, the sooner he'd get what he was waiting for.

There had been no clues in Bhaki's text – just a request to see him.

A message from Lauren had been more revealing. Their best lead so far had turned out to be nothing more than a waste of time.

The team would be getting frustrated, tempers would fray and the odd sharp word would be spoken. There had been no mention of pressure from DCI Grantham, but Evans knew it would be applied before much longer.

He was never good at waiting. After five minutes, he was pacing his lounge like an expectant father; the book he'd been reading was left open on the arm of his chair. Tripod watched him pace, his head moving left to right like a front-row spectator at Wimbledon.

Evans stopped his march and put on the kettle, got a couple of plates from the cupboard and lit a cigarette.

As he was making the coffee, it struck him that he didn't know how Bhaki took his. All the time he'd been on his team, he'd never once made him a cuppa, or paid attention when the lad was telling someone else.

It struck him that he'd been selfish and uncaring about a lot of aspects in his team. The more he thought about it, the greater his self-loathing became. He felt he should make amends, but he wasn't sure how to go about it.

A knock sounded at the door. Evans let Bhaki in, and tried to hide the growling from his stomach behind a cough. When the message had come in requesting his help, Bhaki had said he'd bring food.

Evans had hoped Bhaki would collect something from his parents' restaurant, and he wasn't disappointed.

Bhaki passed over the bag of food. 'Mum said to say hi.'

For once, Evans left his bottle of Tabasco sauce where it sat. Bhaki's mother's cooking was filled with enough flavours to not need any further enhancement.

The Bhaki family had moved to Carlisle in the early eighties, and within three years had the busiest restaurant in town. She ran her kitchen like a military operation, while Bhaki's father charmed diners and drove his staff to Michelin levels of service. Evans dined there at least once a month – more often since Janet died.

Bhaki's mother refused to do takeaway food for customers, but family members would always be able to get something from her. There wasn't a menu for family, she would serve them whatever she had to hand or could knock up in a hurry.

Tonight's meal was a medley of vegetable bhajis, spiced pakoras and a chicken curry containing chickpeas, spinach and green chillies.

The food was too good for Evans to talk around, so he parked his impatience until both plates had been wiped clean with the last of the chapatis.

'Tell your mother that was the best meal she's ever made me when you see her next.' Evans reached for his wallet. 'What do I owe you?'

'Nothing. She never charges me and, when she heard it was for you, she told me not to take a penny from you.'

Evans made a mental note to do something nice for Bhaki's mother the next time he dined in their restaurant.

'Right then. Spill it. Your bribe for my expertise has been consumed and thoroughly enjoyed. It's time to get down to business.'

As Bhaki brought him up to date on their progress so far, Evans listened without interrupting. It was only after Bhaki explained his theory that he spoke.

'So, you think this is connected to the boy rather than her sex life?' Evans flicked ash from his cigarette into the ashtray sitting atop a nest of tables. 'From what you've told me, it looks very much as if there wasn't much of an investigation into the boy's dealing.'

'Exactly. I think the boy stashed the money he'd made somewhere. I just can't figure out why his mother was stabbed.'

Bhaki flapped a hand in frustration. 'Or had something cut out of her stomach.'

Evans felt the blood whoosh through his veins as ideas bounced around his head. This kind of brainstorming was something he loved, and in the few days, since he'd been retired, he'd missed it far more than he'd ever admit.

'In light of the quality of your mother's cooking, I'll skip the part where I insult your intelligence. This is what I think may have happened: the boy had entrusted the money to his mother and someone came calling for it. That someone gave her a couple of slaps to soften her up. She was made of sterner stuff and swallowed the key to wherever the money was stashed. The mysterious someone, or someones, then decided not to wait for nature to take its course and instead played a twisted version of doctors and nurses.'

Bhaki's eyes flashed with excitement as he spoke. 'I think you're right, guv.'

'So do I. You'll need to go see the boy. Put some pressure on him. I'd suggest you make sure Lauren is with you. The boy is sixteen years old and is bound to be as horny as fuck – he probably hasn't seen a good-looking woman for months unless one of the probation officers is a young hottie. One flash of Lauren's stocking top, or a look down her blouse, will have him telling you everything before he realises he's said too much.'

'Maybe I should just slowly flick through a wank mag instead of taking Lauren. Perhaps that'd be less insulting to her.'

Evans returned Bhaki's smile. 'You try and tell Lauren that's what you're going to do. Twenty pence says she'll tell you to bugger off and leave her to do her job.'

'You'd win your twenty pence.'

Chapter 21

As he waited by the school reception for Jack's head of year, Bhaki looked around and saw how much school had changed since his day. That familiar antiseptic smell of cleaning fluids still competed with sweat and hormones, but there was a level of security that he'd never experienced as a pupil.

Now it was all locked doors and numbered keypads. If the kids were anything like those he'd gone to school with, it would be a matter of hours before the codes were learned for each door. The pupils might not remember much about calculus, split infinitives, or which Roman emperor followed Julius Caesar, but they'd know every security code by heart.

As the minutes dragged on, Bhaki couldn't help feeling like a naughty child awaiting a meeting with the headmaster. He'd only once been in enough trouble for such a thing to happen, but the disappointment on his mother's face was etched into his memory.

A stern looking woman strode around the corner and approached him with a handout and the kind of expression that suggested she'd better things to do than answer his questions. 'DC Bhaki? I'm Sam Fowler.'

'Thank you for seeing me. I'll try not to take up too much of your time.' Bhaki planned to use politeness to win her over. Evans may have used confrontation as a way to take control of situations, but he couldn't bring himself to be rude when there were other options.

He'd expected a man, after seeing the name Sam Fowler in the report, but he knew he shouldn't have made assumptions. He pushed away the unkind thought that her mannish posture and dress sense would be a huge source of playground ridicule should the pupils learn her Christian name.

'Thanks.' Her frostiness thawed by a degree or two. 'What can I help you with?'

'I'm looking into Jack Simon's arrest for dealing drugs. There are some aspects which I'm not sure add up.'

Another three degrees of frost fell away. 'I heard what happened to his mother. That poor woman, and poor, poor Gracie. I'll tell you what I can, but I don't think I can add anything I haven't already told your colleagues.'

'I've read the statement you gave at the time.' Bhaki chose his words with care. 'I got the impression you were surprised Jack was caught with that amount of drugs.'

'I was.' She gave a grimacing side nod. 'Being honest with you, you can suss most of your class out in a few lessons. You know which ones are likely to end up pregnant, or addicted to some drug or other. You can tell which ones will go on to make a success of their lives, and those who'll be nothing more than a burden to society.'

'And which category did Jack fall into?'

'I figured he'd go on to do something worthwhile. He wasn't the most outgoing but, by the same token, he was well-mannered and as obedient as you can hope any teenage boy will be. If he hadn't been caught with the drugs, I'd have guessed he'd go on to find some kind of job that allowed him to work either on his own or in a small team.' Her eyes clouded. 'Most kids gain confidence as they age, but Jack was the opposite. The longer I knew him, the more he became withdrawn.'

'Were there any incidents he was involved in?'

'None that I'm aware of. He didn't bother with anyone except Olly Dawson. The two of them were inseparable. Neither were involved in any fights, or bullying, or trouble other than the usual "dog-ate-my-homework" kind of thing.'

Bhaki remembered the boy's statement. 'What's Olly like?'

'He's just like Jack; only since Jack was arrested he's become even more withdrawn. He doesn't speak to anyone. He just hangs out by himself and does what he needs to do to get by in class. His grades have dropped but not so much that he's likely to fail. It's as if he's just doing the bare minimum.'

Bhaki paused for a moment's reflection. It wasn't just the villains who suffered when they went to jail. Their friends and family all paid a price for believing in someone and loving them. Like victims, they were usually innocent, but that didn't mean they went unpunished. He'd seen countless mothers, wives and children leave court with tear-stained faces after their loved ones had been incarcerated. Husbands and fathers would have stoic expressions and glassy eyes as they tried to comfort the inconsolable.

'Do you know if Jack got on well with any of the teachers – if there were any he may have confided in?'

'He did an after-school club which was run by Mr Booth and Mr Talbot.' A look to the ceiling as she trawled her memory. 'I think it was some kind of engineering class.'

'Thanks for all your help. Do you think I could speak with them?'

She looked at her watch. 'There'll be a break in quarter of an hour. I'll arrange for them to come and see you.'

Chapter 22

Campbell pulled up to the gate and showed his warrant card to the guard. The large mesh gate opened in front of him.

As soon as he'd finished speaking with Bhaki last night, he'd put in a call to Deerbolt and requested a morning appointment with Jack Simon.

He'd brought Lauren with him and they'd gone over the list of questions they'd put to Jack. She had them written up in her neat handwriting, but he was aware they'd have to adapt to whatever Jack said.

Lauren had pouted and fallen silent when he'd told her to reign in her seductive ways. Jack Simon might be sixteen, but he was in a young offenders institution. Any reports of her using sexuality to trick him wouldn't reflect well on either of them.

He figured Bhaki had spoken to her last night, as she wore a white blouse sheer enough to show the lacy red bra she wore beneath it.

His request that she keep her coat on had been met with a harrumphed compliance.

It took twenty minutes of security checks and waiting around, but they eventually found themselves walking into an interview room.

The boy rose to his feet as soon as they entered. 'How's my mum? They won't tell me anything here and I can't call my aunt because the phone's busted.'

'I checked with the hospital. She's still in ICU fighting the infection.'

Jack sank back into the lone chair on his side of the table. 'Thank God for that. When I heard you were coming I thought you were going to tell me she'd died.'

Lauren sat opposite him and laid a gentle hand on his arm. 'That's not why we're here.'

'Then why are you here?' Suspicion clouded his eyes.

'We have a few questions for you.'

'What about?' Jack fidgeted in his seat. 'I'm not telling you anything. I don't want to answer your questions.' His eyes flitted to the guard standing by the door. 'Can I go back to my cell please?'

'We think we know why your mother was attacked. We want you to help us confirm our theory.'

Campbell watched the boy's face display a range of emotions before settling on confusion. The interview room was warm but the boy's face had no colour other than a fading black eye. As he waited for curiosity to get the better of Jack, he felt a bead of sweat trickle down his back.

'How can I know anything about the attack when I've been stuck in here?'

Lauren's tone was kept at a respectful, conversational level. 'We think your mum was attacked for your money. We think she hid it somewhere for you and, when the person you owe money came for it, she swallowed the key. They cut into her stomach and retrieved the key. If you tell us who you owe money, we can arrest them and put them in jail.'

'I don't owe anyone any money.' The reply was no more than a whisper. 'I had nothing to do with those drugs – have never bought or sold any drugs.'

'It's time for you to tell us the truth, Jack.'

His head moved side to side in slow, deliberate movements.

'Don't you want your mother's attacker locked up? What kind of a son do you think you are, when you don't have the guts to point the finger at the person who cut your mother open? Don't you know she did what she did to protect you?' Campbell stood and made for the door. 'C'mon, let's leave this spineless piece of shit to sit in his cell all day thinking how much he's let his mother down.'

Lauren stood and peeled off her jacket. Hung it on the back of her chair and sat down again. 'You go if you want, sir. I think you're underestimating Jack, and I'm prepared to wait until he makes the right decision.'

Campbell scowled at her and dumped himself back in his seat. Lauren taking her jacket off hadn't been part of their plan. He'd kept his eyes on Jack – throughout his false rant and while Lauren had removed her jacket – and the boy had barely looked at her. Had no interest in looking at her chest.

His disinterest may stem from his mind being elsewhere, or because his taste lay in another direction, but his reaction was unusual. In here there would be no privacy for him to relieve his sexual frustration. Lauren was a beautiful woman and, dressed as she was, she warranted a once over from any male – let alone one who'd been cooped up in a place where he couldn't easily have a ham shank.

Beside him, he could tell Lauren was struggling with the boy's offhand rejection of her sexuality. To her, Jack's disinterest was a personal slight.

Campbell had to give Lauren her due: she kept her tone level and face soft as she tried again. 'Who's going to be right, Jack? Me for having faith that you'll do the right thing, or DI Campbell for thinking you're too gutless to give us the name of the person who plunged a knife into your mother's stomach?'

'Can't.'

The word came out as little more than a breath, but Campbell heard it.

'You can, Jack.' Lauren laid her hand on his arm again. 'You tell us who you think attacked your mother and we'll be able to take them off the streets so your mother and sister are safe. Tell us where you got the drugs from and you'll be able to prevent your family suffering another attack.'

'It wasn't drugs.'

'Then what did your mother swallow?'

Jack's eyes fell to the floor and his voice became a self-conscious mutter.

'A locker key.'

'What was in the locker?'

'Proof.'

Chapter 23

Mr Booth was a tall man with a slight frame. His accent was local and he had the air of authority of someone used to being obeyed. Beside him, Mr Talbot's bulging gut made him look as if he'd been sired by a pair of space hoppers.

'Thank you for giving up your break to speak to me. I believe you ran an after-school club that Jack Simon attended?'

'That's right.' Booth spoke for them. 'It was such a shame he turned out to be dealing drugs. It caught me by surprise, I have to say.'

'That seems to be the general consensus. Can you tell me your impression of him?'

'He was a good kid who must have got in with the wrong crowd.' Booth wiped his fingers on his sleeve. 'I would never have thought he'd have done that. What about you, Doug?'

Talbot's accent told Bhaki that the man had been born within sight of the Tyne Bridge. He looked to be less affable than his colleague and his tone suggested bored irritation.

'He was alright in class, I'll give him that much, but I have to say I had my suspicions about him.'

'In what way?' Bhaki fought to keep the excitement from his voice. This could be the breakthrough he was after.

'I've seen his type before. They have one or two friends at most, and they hang around the playground not taking part in football matches or any of the other games. They don't fit into any of the natural groups that form and, as such, they become outcasts. Being the go-to source for drugs makes them popular.'

Bhaki caught the look the teachers exchanged.

'What about you, Mr Booth, would you agree with Mr Talbot's assessment?'

'To a point.' A wry smile and another wiping of his hands on his jacket sleeves. 'He's spent more time teaching in schools in deprived areas than I have, so I'd have to bow to his superior experience.'

Bhaki was puzzled by the wiping habit. It was akin to the constant washing of the hands – which was a positive indicator of a guilt complex.

'So, you think there's a strong chance he was guilty of supplying drugs to other children?'

'The drugs were found in his locker and the court found him guilty. I'm not sure my opinion really counts but, for the record, while I was surprised in one sense, I've learned the hard way not to be surprised by anything kids get up to.'

'He's right you know. We've currently got two fourteen-year-olds and one thirteen-year-old who're pregnant.' His top lip pulled into a sneer. 'All the female teachers under forty have had their arse pinched by a student and most of them have had their breasts squeezed. Just yesterday, a first-year pupil put a hunting knife against the throat of someone who pinched a chip from their plate at lunchtime.'

'You make this sound like a problem school.'

A shrug from Booth. 'It's no worse than any other school whose intake includes a high proportion of children who're from single-parent families, or families where unemployment is a choice.'

Bhaki got the picture at once. The nearby Harraby estate had more than its fair share of families who fit either of Booth's qualifiers. Harraby may not quite be classified as a sink estate, but there were areas which were among the roughest parts of Carlisle.

When he'd been in uniform, he'd attended callouts to Harraby on a daily basis. There were twenty or so houses they visited with a metronomic regularity. It would be these homes that provided the teen mothers, knife wielders and most of the school bullies. Their occupants were the type who settled disputes with fists and threats. Stolen goods would pass through the houses, as would every drug known to man. There would be uneasy truces with rival families on other estates, and the only people who could exert any real kind of authority over them would be the Leightons, as there was no respect for law and order.

'Did you ever see Jack hanging out with any of the kids from the ... ah ... problem families?'

'He only ever hung with his mate Olly, but he was a polite lad who'd speak when spoken to. If one of the other kids spoke to him, he'd answer them.'

A bell sounded and Bhaki saw both men look at their watches. 'Is there anything else you can tell me, gentlemen?'

Talbot shook his head. 'I'd just say that, as noble as your intentions may be, in my opinion, you're wasting your time. The lad was caught fair and square and he was sent to a young offenders institution by the courts.'

Bhaki watched as the teachers hurried off to their classes. His thoughts fixed on Booth's version of handwashing, and Talbot's final statement.

He had enough doubts to raise the matter with Campbell when he returned to the office. Perhaps a formal interview under caution would shake them enough to loosen whatever they may be hiding.

Chapter 24

Jack lifted his T-shirt up to his face and wiped his eyes for perhaps the tenth time. Beside him, Campbell could see his own horror reflected in Lauren's eyes as they listened to what Jack was telling them.

'You say you were abused by two of your teachers. What are their names?'

Campbell wasn't sure he could keep the emotion from his voice the way Lauren was. All he could think of was his own infant son growing up to endure the same torment. At least Alan would have a father he could go to with such problems. Anyone who did such a thing to his son wouldn't be meeting John Campbell as a detective inspector. They'd be meeting him as a murderous father.

'Mr Talbot and Mr Booth.' A sniff. 'I have proof.'

'It's awesome that you have proof of what they're doing, but it's a very serious allegation you're making. I'd like you to tell me the full story – starting at the beginning.' Lauren fished a tissue from her bag and handed it to Jack. 'It's not that I don't believe you because I do, I just need to understand the sequence of events.'

'The first time was when Olly and me were clearing away our stuff after the engineering session. There was only the two of us and Mr Booth. He was showing us a design he wanted us to consider making the next week, and we were sat either side of him.' Another sniff was accompanied by a wiping of his eyes with the tissue. 'He put his hands on our knees and slid them up until they almost touched our balls. It was horrible.'

'I'm sure it was. What happened next?'

'Nothing. We just left. Both me and Olly were shocked. We couldn't believe it had happened.'

Campbell clenched and unclenched his fists beneath the table as he listened to Jack detail how the abuse had worsened each week. Both boys had been groped by Talbot and Booth over a six month period.

When Lauren had asked why they'd never reported it, he'd lifted a shoulder and said that Booth had threatened to rape Gracie, and Olly's sister if they told anyone or stopped coming to the after-school class.

On and on Jack went, every word uttered carrying the ring of truth. His voice wavered, then found strength before wavering again, as he went through the whole sordid ordeal.

'In the end, me and Olly knew we'd have to find a way to stop them ourselves.'

'What did you do?' Campbell noted the catch in Lauren's voice. 'How did you stop them?'

'We saved our dinner money for a month and used it to buy a surveillance camera. It was one of the thin ones you could poke through a lock. We tossed a coin. I lost. Olly pretended to be sick then went to school for the last period. He waited outside the classroom until the engineering course was over, and then he filmed Mr Booth and Mr Talbot abusing me.' Jack set his jaw into a determined position. 'We made two copies of the footage and loaded it on to two memory sticks and my phone. We confronted them, one by one, showed them the footage. Told them we'd go to the police if they didn't stop abusing us.'

'Did they stop?'

'The next day, I saw Olly. He'd been stupid and had kept his memory stick in his schoolbag. It went missing during a normal class Mr Booth was teaching.' A sniff. 'I tricked the school secretary, by giving a false name, and I managed to hire a second locker at the school. I put my memory stick in there and hid the key in my bedroom.'

'What happened then?'

'I went to school as normal and that's when the drugs were found in my locker.'

'Did you tell your mum about it?'

'No.' Jack's head shook violently. 'I couldn't tell her what they'd done to me. Couldn't tell anyone. There's no way I could testify in court. Olly is the same. We had to stop them ourselves and then try and lead normal lives.'

'How did your mother get the key?'

'I gave it to her before my court case. I knew I was going to end up in here if I didn't grass them up. I didn't tell her what it was for, or anything like that. I just told her that she must keep it safe and never give it to anyone but me.'

Campbell didn't have to ask why Jack had kept silent and taken the fall. The boy was out of his depth and was terrified for his sister's safety. There was also the ordeal of having to testify in court. For a youngster like him, to stand up and admit to having been abused would be unthinkable when the easier option was to keep his mouth shut and escape the torment of his teachers.

'You've been very brave telling us all this. I'll make sure that, when this comes to court, your name will not be released to the papers; we'll have you out of here as soon as possible. I'm sure the education authorities will be able to find you a place in a school in another part of town.'

Campbell's voice was gruffer than he wanted it to be, but he blamed that on hiding his anger at the teachers and sadness for the boy.

He'd been wrong when he thought he saw fear in Jack's eyes. It was the horror of having endured abuse at the hands of someone who was supposed to be a positive influence and a guardian of morality. The knowledge of how his mother had tried to protect him would play on his mind as he lay on his prison bunk tonight.

Chapter 25

Evans' injuries made it a struggle for him to match the pace set by the headmaster, but there was no way he was going to show any kind of weakness. At his side, Bhaki was as grim-faced as he'd ever seen him.

The headmaster was an upright man whose shoulders were bunched with stress. His face showed his disgust and Evans knew the man would be bolstering himself for the forthcoming investigation into the school, and his reign as headmaster.

A janitor stood, beside the row of lockers, with a set of skeleton keys in his hand and a curious expression on his lined face.

The headmaster gave the janitor the locker number and they all watched as he selected a key and opened the locker door.

It was bare. Empty. The headmaster gave an audible sigh of relief – which he cut off when he saw Bhaki glowering at him.

Evans felt pride in the young Asian. Not only was he proving to be an excellent detective, he was starting to exert his personality on to others. As much as he wanted to berate the headmaster himself, doing so wouldn't be wise. He was here on sufferance rather than in any official capacity.

The locker being empty was a blow, but they had expected it to be. After the lengths Booth and Talbot had gone to getting the key, they would have retrieved the memory stick at the earliest opportunity.

Both men were now in custody and their electronic devices were being examined by Chisholm. Any trace of abusive images of children would support Jack's statement.

A family liaison officer had been brought in to speak with Olly and his parents. Once his statement was added to Jack's, the evidence would begin to mount.

The headmaster looked bewildered now that the locker was shown to be empty. Evans had little empathy for the man. While he wasn't directly responsible for Talbot and Booth's misuse of their positions, Evans felt he had to carry some blame for the misdemeanours of his staff. When he'd run the Major Crimes Team, he'd always held the view that the captain was responsible for the actions of everyone on the ship.

'So,' the headmaster looked at Bhaki. 'What happens now?'

'We'll conduct a full investigation into the allegations that have been made. We'll need to speak to all of your staff over the coming weeks.'

'I don't mean to be impolite, but aren't you rather junior to be running this investigation?'

Evans stepped between Bhaki and the headmaster before the young detective could give an answer. His forefinger jabbed at the headmaster's chest. 'Are you taking the piss? He's the one whose investigative skills uncovered a terrible crime that's happened on your watch. His direct boss is on his way back from taking a statement from a victim of child abuse. This victim was abused here – in this very school – again under your watch. As far as DC Bhaki's presence goes, consider it the opening skirmishes of a war that's about to go global. By the end of the day, there will be DCIs, chief constables and every other rank of copper you can think of, crawling all over this school.' Evans waved his hand around his head. 'I reckon this place will be on all the news channels by tomorrow evening at the latest. Someone, somewhere, will say the wrong thing to the wrong person and the press will get wind and you'll have reporters doing pieces to camera outside. So, if I was you, I'd be more concerned with calling whoever it is you answer to, before they hear it on the news. Trust me, the age and rank of the person in front of you has no bearing whatsoever on the size of the shit-storm that's coming your way.'

The headmaster blanched in the face of his diatribe, but Evans didn't care. The man had bigger problems to face, and his attempt to belittle Bhaki as the source of his woes wasn't something he could stand by and watch.

Evans felt a strong hand on his arm as Bhaki pushed him aside.

'Mr Evans is correct, Headmaster. All of that is going to happen. If these allegations are proven, then I should imagine you'll be extremely lucky to keep your job.' Bhaki moved forward until his nose was an inch from the headmaster's. 'If it was up to me, I'd have you sent down with your teachers for your failure to protect the pupils in your school. I might only be a DC, I might only be twenty-four, but in the last forty-eight hours I've done far more to protect your pupils than you have. So I'd suggest you fuck off back to your office, call your boss and grovel like you've never grovelled before because if you stay around here insulting me, I'm likely to arrest you on the same charges as your teachers.'

The headmaster stalked away with his head and shoulders drooping in defeat.

Evans took Bhaki's arm and walked towards the exit. 'C'mon you. Come with me.'

Once they were outside, Evans lit a cigarette and stood in the drizzle with Bhaki.

'Don't say it, guv. Just … don't … say it.'

Evans hadn't been going to say anything, so he just waited and smoked until Bhaki was ready to look his way. The outburst and threat had been a flashing neon sign in terms of how Bhaki was handling this case. Paedophilia was the most heinous of crimes and, while his own emotions were running high, Bhaki was closer to the investigation than he was. He'd comforted the victim's sister as their mother fought for her life; been dogged in his investigating and bright enough to work out the solution to the original case.

The fact there was a hidden element couldn't have been foreseen, but it was his work that had brought it to light.

'Shit, guv. I was so close to hitting him.'

'You didn't though, did you?' Evans lit another cigarette from the butt of the first. 'I'd have chinned him if I was in your shoes. You should be proud of your restraint and proud of your work. It's absolutely shite what you found, but it needed finding and you found it.'

Bhaki made a dismissive noise and took a kick at a coke can probably dropped by an uncaring pupil.

'I mean it. You should be proud of yourself.' Evans pulled on his cigarette. 'I'm proud of you.'

Chapter 26

Campbell took a seat beside Lauren as she recited the necessary details for the device recording the interview.

Across the table, Eddie Booth looked scared and sullen. His posture spoke of bravado, but his eyes showed how he really felt.

Both he and Lauren had taken a walk around the outside of the police station. The drizzle had permeated their clothing and turned Lauren's hair frizzy, but they hadn't minded. She'd smoked and he'd stomped his anger away. It took three laps of the building before they felt calm enough to conduct the interview.

On their way back from Deerbolt, Lauren had released more than a few tears and he'd found himself possessed by the worst case of road rage he'd ever experienced.

He was wise enough to recognise that their heightened emotional state was due to hearing Jack's story and seeing the pain on his face as he told it. As soon as he'd organised the arrests of both teachers, he'd called his wife and told her to give their son a kiss from him. It wasn't enough to lessen his anger, but it was the best he could do at the time. He'd wanted to hug Jack – soothe his agony and promise a better future – but he knew better than to have physical contact with an inmate.

'The charges you are levelling at my client, do you have proof for them?'

Booth's lawyer was a duty solicitor. He'd never met Francis Kendrick but had disliked the smarmy prig at first sight. The man's unctuous tone was that of a snake-oil salesman. The most telling thing about him was that Lauren had nipped to the ladies and put a slip beneath her blouse. This made him think she'd encountered Kendrick before and had come off second best. The extra layer beneath her blouse made Campbell suspect a formal complaint about Lauren's clothing may have been lodged in the past.

'We have a statement from one victim. A member of our team and a family liaison officer are taking a statement from another as we speak, and then there's the search history on your computer.'

'Don't forget the messages between Mr Booth and Mr Talbot, DC Phillips. We have those too.'

The glance Kendrick flicked towards Booth was one of disdain and abandonment. All lawyers knew a losing case when they saw one.

'Let me get this straight. Allegations of paedophilia have been made and you say you have evidence to back them up. Where does the attempted murder charge fit in, and what evidence do you have of that?'

Lauren's voice was cool but professional. 'We have the message chain between your client and Mr Talbot in which they discuss going to visit Mrs Simon with the express purpose of retrieving Jack's memory stick.'

'I'm sorry, but I find that hard to believe. Jack Simon was arrested months ago. If, as you suggest, my client did want to retrieve a memory stick that held evidence against him, I would ask you why he waited more than six months to get it?' Kendrick's head shook. 'That doesn't make sense to me.'

'It didn't to us either. That's why we asked Jack if he knew why there was such a delay between events.'

'And his reasoning?'

'He told us that he'd sent the teacher a letter, reminding him about the evidence, when he heard that his little sister was being taught by your client. We think being reminded of the memory stick was too much for your client. We think it was enough to send him round to the Simon's house.' Lauren's eyes moved to Booth. 'Is that the case, Mr Booth?'

'No comment.'

Kendrick's gaze was level. 'Okay, so you reckon he's got a motive for being there. It still doesn't explain why you're levelling an attempted murder charge at him though.'

Lauren's answer was interrupted by a knock at the door, followed by the entry of Chisholm.

Campbell took the sheet of paper Chisholm was carrying, and scanned it before passing it over to Lauren.

'Well, Mr Booth, it seems you're full of surprises.' Campbell relished the fear in Booth's eyes as he spoke. 'Those years you spent training to be a doctor must have come in very useful when you cut into Mrs Simon's stomach. The surgeon who saved Mrs Simon's life said the cut was very precise, and that it showed surgical skill. Do you have anything to say?'

'No comment.'

'In that case, we're going to charge you with the attempted murder of Julie Simon. Once you've been charged you'll be detained while we gather more evidence of your paedophilia. I'm sure Mr Kendrick will hang around to consult with you. I should imagine he'll advise you to save the public an expensive trial by pleading guilty, in the hope it will earn you a little less jail time.'

Chapter 27

Evans stood by the door and looked over the team. Despite the fact they'd just got a good result, there were none of the usual celebrations for a case being closed.

Papers were shuffled and reports were filled in, as they all made sure everything was in order.

ACC Greg Hadley had just left, after thanking the team for their efforts. His praise had received nothing more than polite nods, as the team were smarting at the news that he'd called in a specialist team to investigate the teachers' behaviour.

The Serious and Organised Crime Agency might be the UK's answer to the FBI, but it was the team, and Bhaki in particular, who'd exposed the paedophiles. Having the case taken off them was a slap in the face.

A counterbalance to this was the fact they'd all sleep easier if their days weren't spent dealing with such a sordid case. The public couldn't, and probably shouldn't, know how much investigating certain crimes took from coppers. How there were sleepless nights and nightmares when sleep did come. How relationships failed and how solace was sought at the bottom of a bottle. Sometimes coppers chose drink, and sometimes drink chose them.

The ringing of Bhaki's mobile cut across the office, but none of the other three looked up.

Evans watched as Bhaki listened to the caller, spoke a couple of words, and then laid his mobile down with gentle care.

The young detective's head slumped forward and he saw a series of splashes on the desk as fat tears fell.

He gave him a minute or two and then walked over, laid a gentle hand on his shoulder and gave a supportive squeeze. 'What is it, Amir?' He could guess at the answer, but he knew Bhaki well enough to know the tears wouldn't be for himself.

'It's Julie Simon. She passed away twenty minutes ago.'

Thank you for reading *No Comment*

We hope you enjoyed it and would consider leaving a review of the book or a rating. It means so much to authors and publishers to get feedback about our books, so we can improve them and keep delivering books you love. All our books are professionally edited and proofread by our editorial team, however, occasionally a mistake might slip through. If you do find something, we hope that this would not spoil your enjoyment of the book but please make a note of it and send the details through to info@caffeinenights.com and we will amend it and ensure we give you something in return for your efforts.

Caffeine Nights Newsletter

If you would like to know more about the next Graham Smith book or any of our other authors or books, please sign up for our free newsletter at www.caffeinenights.com. Your email address and details are completely safe with us and never passed on or sold to anyone else and there is an unsubscribe link in every email should you choose you no longer want to receive our newsletter. All new newsletter subscribers can download a free eBook too.

We love social media and tweeting or posting on Facebook or putting a pic on Instagram is a great way to tell folks what you have enjoyed. You can follow us at:

Twitter - @caffeinenights

Facebook - Caffeine Nights

Instagram @ Caffeinenights

And if you share anything about our books we will share with our followers.

Read the new DI Harry Evans novel

When the Waters Recede

Two dead bodies, one evil woman, one mystery man

When a car is pulled from raging floodwaters with a dead man in the front and the decapitated body of an evil woman in the boot, Cumbria's Major Crimes Team are handed the investigation.

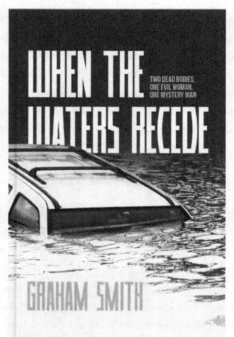

The woman is soon recognised, but the man cannot be identified, and this leads the team and their former leader, Harry Evans, into areas none of them want to visit.

Before they know it, they're dealing with protection scams and looking for answers to questions they didn't know needed to be asked.